NOMAD

Sons of Sanctuary MC
Book 3

Victoria Danann

Copyright © 2017 Victoria Danann
Published by 7th House Publishing
Imprint of Andromeda LLC

Read more about this author and upcoming works at
VictoriaDanann.com

CHAPTER ONE

Cannon Johns was soaking wet when he pulled into the motel. Mid October rain storms are the worst.

The vacancy light was on, but the once-bright neon was burned out on the first "A" and the second "C". He was bone weary, out of options, and hungry, which was why his attention was drawn to the vending machine sitting under the overhang, barely out of the driving rain. The whole place was seedy, in disrepair, but he hadn't been expecting a five star hotel with Relais & Châteaux room service.

It was way too late to find food anywhere else in the tiny panhandle town of Barburnett, Texas. He'd passed a Sonic and a convenience store, but both had been put to bed hours before. There was only one option. Three rundown machines. Two selling drinks. One vending the usual assortment of candy, crackers, pretzels and other unsatisfying stuff guaranteed to hasten demise. Which would be okay with him.

He unlocked the door marked with a number 16 and rolled his Harley inside. He hadn't gotten permission, but didn't expect the guy at the front desk would object. The man's Indian accent was so thick Cann had been forced to ask him to repeat himself several times. The night manager, who was probably also the owner, gave every indication of being a man who wouldn't be presenting much of an obstacle to anything that came his way. Especially not when cash was involved.

Kickstand set in place, Cannon promised himself that he'd towel off his ride as soon as he'd put on dry clothes and stuffed some empty calories into his stomach. He was never so glad that he'd taken the time to cover his clothes in plastic before stowing them in the side containers affectionately called saddle bags. Even the tightest, newest, best-made bike could leak in a hard enough rain and, at that moment, he would have said he needed dry clothes every bit as much as food or drink.

First order of business, vending machines.

Stepping back out into the hundred percent humidity air, he stayed close to the building on the part of the walkway that was under the overhang and dry. Not that it mattered. He couldn't be any *more* wet. Out of habit, he looked around before starting toward the lighted food and drink dispensers. He was almost there when he saw movement by the Mountain Dew column. Somebody was crouched behind the one furthest from the rain, with the most darkness for cover.

In addition to being tired, hungry, and out of options, he was also out of sorts, with no patience for shenanigans, a combination that could play out very badly for a would-be mugger. Weary as he was, he wouldn't mind a good excuse for administering some bare knuckle punishment to the wicked.

When he was eight feet away from the Mountain Dew column, he said, "Come on out of there and state your business." He had to raise his voice to a near-shout to be heard over the pounding rain.

After a slight hesitation, a small figure emerged in a yellow plastic poncho, the kind you can get at the grocery store for a couple of bucks. As soon as she reached up to pull the hood back he knew it was a woman by the delicate size of her hands and the way she moved.

The light was dim, but he saw her as clearly as if it was noon on a bright sunny day. His late wife had once told him that he had to change out the light fixture in the kitchen because "nobody looks good in fluorescent light". The girl standing in front of him was proof it just ain't so.

Her eyes were violet blue. And wide. He wasn't sure if that was because of fear or misery. Like him, she was soaking wet. Unlike him, she was shivering. Whether that was from fear or cold he couldn't tell for sure.

"What the hell you doing out here, girl?" He looked around. "Somethin' got you spooked?"

She licked her bottom lip. "No, I… ah, I'm just a little down on luck. I don't want any trouble."

"Don't want no trouble, huh." It wasn't a question. He said it as if it was a provable fact. She shook her head to both punctuate his assessment and agree with it. "Yeah. Me neither. At least not tonight."

He fed the dollar bills he'd gotten from the night

manager into the machine one by one, selecting items that were fried and coated in cheese that was more chemical than dairy, or candy bars that were more sugar than protein. When he held a Snickers out to the girl, she took it.

He breathed the rainy air deep into his lungs and let it out slowly. "Well, come on. You can't spend the night out here." When she didn't move to follow, he said, "If your woman's intuition is sayin' I might do you harm, it's badly in need of a tune up."

She continued to simply stare. She was either frozen by her resolve to stay put or frozen by indecision. Either way she wasn't moving.

"Have it your way," he said and started back toward his room.

After taking three steps he heard the rustle of plastic poncho over the rain and knew she was behind him. He'd left his room unlocked knowing that he'd only be gone a couple of minutes and that the door would be in sight the entire time. Not that anybody besides himself and the lost girl would be out in that little forgotten town at that time of night, in that weather.

He pushed open the door, turned on the overhead light, and looked around, realizing what the place would look like in her eyes.

Two double beds covered in old rose chenille spreads. He refused to think about whether or not they'd been washed since the last occupant or occupants. At least the sheets were clean.

The walls were covered in pecan-stained faux paneling left over from the seventies. The carpet was a ratty rust color, but that was okay. Even he knew it would be rude to park his bike on carpet if it was nice and new.

He turned on the two bedside table lamps, which gave the room a slightly less down-and-out look.

The girl still stood outside on the walkway. Her toes were touching the threshold, but it seemed she still hadn't made up her mind about what she was going to do.

"In or out, girl. Makes no difference to me. But one way or the other that door is about to close."

When he started back toward the door, she took a step inside and moved to the right out of the way of the closing door, watching him like he'd been on the news as an escaped psycho killer.

He pulled off his leather jacket that displayed the Sons of Sanctuary logo on the back, closed the door, locked it, and stomped off toward the bath to get a towel for drying off the bike, stopping by the thermostat on the way to turn up the heat.

He returned with two glasses and a towel, which he set on the seat before opening one of the compartments. He withdrew clothes and a fifth of bourbon.

"Which bed do you want?" he asked.

She looked at the two beds with trepidation, but didn't answer.

"Okay, then. I'll take that one." He pointed at the bed closest to the door.

He divided up the vending machine haul. Two candy

bars on top of his bedspread. Two candy bars on top of the other bedspread. Two chips on each. Two cheese and peanut butter crackers on each.

Setting the glasses next to each other on the table by the ancient console TV, he poured an inch of bourbon into each glass. "This will warm you up." He downed his in one gulp then set the other glass on the bedside table that wasn't his.

"When I finish taking care of my ride," he went on, "I'm going to get a hot shower and put on some dry clothes. Do you have anything dry?" Apparently she was hiding some kind of shoulder bag under the poncho. She lifted it up slightly in silent response. "Okay. Well. You can use the shower after me and put on dry stuff. You got a name?"

She cleared her throat and answered so quietly that Cann almost didn't understand. "Bud."

"What's that?"

"Bud," she said a little louder.

"Look, if you don't want to tell me your name, just say, 'Fuck off,' but don't make up something stupid."

Before he turned back to toweling off the Harley, he thought he saw a tiny burst of flame in eyes that looked too old and tired for her face.

"It's not stupid. It's my name."

He looked up at her and cocked an eyebrow. "If you're on the level, then I guess I should apologize. You just don't strike me as a 'Bud'."

"My daddy… I guess he wanted somebody else."

Cann looked her over. "Why don't you take that thing off? Eat something. Gulp down that bourbon over there. You don't need to be afraid of me. My name's Cannon, but people usually just say Cann." Before she realized that she'd let her guard down a little, he saw a small smile. "What's funny?"

"Uh, nothin'. It's just that your name is kind of…"

"Kind of what?"

"Kind of stupid, too."

Cann stared at her for a few beats before shaking his head. "You got an odd way of accepting hospitality. How old are you?"

"Twenty-five."

"The hell. You are not twenty-five. Gonna ask again, but I hate repeatin' myself. How old are you?"

Her shoulders sagged. "Seventeen."

"Yeah. Sounds more like it."

He glanced over after she pulled the wet poncho over her head. She looked around for a place to hang it and finally settled on spreading it out on the floor.

She was tiny. At six feet two he outweighed her by almost a hundred pounds. He didn't have any trouble understanding why somebody that size would be hesitant to accept a bed from a stranger who looked like him.

She was wearing one of those oversized knit shirts and jeans with a hole in one knee. He thought it was more fashion statement than poverty.

Her hair was dirty blonde and natural. All in all, she was entirely too cute to be hiding behind a drink dispenser at a ratty rundown motel.

Out of the corner of his eye he watched her look around the room as if she was deciding what to do. She'd pulled the strap of the shoulder bag over her head so that it was cross-body. He guessed it was easier to carry that way. When she took it off, she let the bag drop on the bed then sat down on the side of the mattress.

Cann could see she was shivering. After he finished toweling off the bike, he pulled a light blanket down from the closet and handed it to the girl before going off to the shower.

She unfolded the blanket and draped it over her shoulders, feeling almost tearful with relief from the cold. It felt like it had been a very long time since she was last warm.

After staring at the glass for a full ten minutes, she decided to take a drink. She spluttered, gasped for air, and almost choked. The stuff tasted like kerosene or the way she imagined kerosene would taste if somebody was dumb enough to do that.

CHAPTER TWO

Cannon Johns closed his eyes and let the hot water stream over his body. He was a man who'd once had the world in his hands. He was a man who'd lost everything in life that was worth having. He'd pulled into the motel looking for the only comfort life still had to offer. The escape of sleep.

The motel had thoughtfully provided two thin towels, neither of which were intended to take care of a man his size. He'd used one of them on his bike, which left one that was dry. He couldn't very well use both towels and leave the girl with none, so he dried himself as best he could with the towel that was already wet. He put on a pair of clean jeans and opened the door to the tiny bath.

Bud was still sitting on the edge of the bed. She'd been watching the bathroom door while he took a shower. He was a very big, very built guy wearing jeans and nothing else, but for God knows what reason she wasn't afraid of him. It was hard to tell how old he was with that beard. He could have been twenty-five. Could have been thirty-five.

"I left you a dry towel," he said in his gruff way as he

stalked toward the bed next to the door. "I'm going to sleep and hopefully I'll sleep hard. If you plan to knife me in my sleep, I'm warning you now that I don't really have anything worth taking."

"I'm not going to knife you in your sleep." He nodded and pulled back the covers. Replaying how that sounded, she decided to append an afterthought. "Or any other time."

"Hmmm?"

"I'm not going to knife you at all."

"Okay," he said as if he had no personal stake in whether she would or wouldn't. He turned away so that his back was to her.

"Cannon."

"Yeah," he said without turning around.

"Thank you."

He didn't reply or even move, but he did listen to the sounds she made as she pulled things out of her little bag and tried to take a shower quietly. It had been a long, long, long time since he'd shared a room with another person.

When she got into bed, he was still awake wondering what her story could be. When she began to snore softly, he was still awake thinking about all the things that could happen to a girl like her.

Inevitably his thoughts turned to his own baby girl. She'd only been three when she died, but he had no trouble imagining how he would have felt about her when she was seventeen. Who would name a daughter Bud?

Bud felt her shoulder being nudged. Once. Again. She cracked her eyes open and, when she realized where she was, scrambled into a sitting position.

"Come on," he said. "Get dressed. We're gonna get you some hot breakfast before I head out."

When she pulled the covers back he saw that she'd slept in her clothes.

She glanced at the clock. Eight. She'd gotten more sleep than she'd had in a while, but would have loved another ten hours or so.

"Okay."

He watched TV while she used the toilet, brushed her teeth, pulled her hair into a ponytail, situated the shoulder bag across her body and looked at him expectantly.

"You know where to eat in this town?"

"No. I'm not, um, from here."

"How'd you get here?"

"Trucker."

"You hitchhiked?" She nodded. He rolled the bike outside. "You ever been on a motorcycle before?"

"No." She looked it over from end to end.

"You ever spent the night in a motel room with a stranger before?"

"No." Her eyes jerked up to his sky-blue gaze.

"Well, it's just like that. Not hard. Just get on behind me, put your feet there, not there," he pointed as he gave instructions, "and hold onto me. We'll find a café open." She straddled the bike behind him. "Like it or not, you have to hold on or you'll fall the hell off."

"Okay." She tentatively put her arms around him, liking the warmth, but not the closeness.

He fired the machine to life and, when he accelerated, she held on tighter. They found a café in the dilapidated two blocks that had once been called downtown. A few pickup trucks were parked outside.

Cannon parked the bike across the street where he could keep an eye on it.

The locals gave the two of them a good long once-over when they entered, but went back to their business after they'd looked their fill.

Cannon held up two fingers.

"Sit wherever you want," said a woman as she passed by with a plate of food in one hand and a coffee carafe in the other.

Bud looked up at Cannon. He motioned for her to pick a spot. She walked to the furthest booth in the back and slid into the seat facing away from the rest of the café. That left Cannon with his back to the wall, able to see everything that happened in the fine establishment, just the spot he would have chosen for himself.

Sitting across the table, it was the first time he'd felt like he had permission to openly stare at the girl who'd spent the night in his room. She was just as beautiful as he'd originally thought. Maybe more so. But the haunted look tugged at his heart.

He had a lot of questions, more than he should. Before he could decide where to start, the waitress set down two mugs and poured coffee without asking if they wanted any or not.

"Mornin' folks," she said as she set two menus down. "Back in a minute."

"Breakfast is on me," Cannon said. "Have whatever you want. Steak and eggs maybe? After last night's dinner we both need real food."

"Thank you," she said. "That's very nice of you."

He watched her study the menu like there was going to be an exam. They gave their orders when the waitress came back.

He turned his mug around a few times before saying, "You want to tell me how you ended up crouching behind a Mountain Dew machine?" She shook her head. "You want to tell me where you're goin'?"

"Haven't decided yet."

"I see. You from around here?"

"No. Are you?"

Her volley question caught him off guard enough to make him smile a little. She saw that he looked a lot younger when he smiled. "I'm the one askin' the questions."

She cocked her head. "Did I agree to that?"

"You did. When you accepted a free bed, shower, and breakfast."

"You didn't say there was a charge."

For a second he was distracted by the unusual color of her eyes and the fact that she didn't look away like most people did when he gave them a full-on stare down.

"What are you doin' after breakfast?"

"Haven't decided yet. How about you?"

"I'm gonna finish the trip I started. Goin' home."

"Where's that?"

"Austin."

"Austin," she repeated. "I've been there. When I was a kid."

He chuckled. "When you were a kid, huh? What is it that you think you are now?"

She looked at him for a long time like she was deciding whether or not to answer and finally said, "Not a kid."

The waitress arrived with two platters that smelled like heaven to both of them. "Did you want gravy with those biscuits?" she asked.

He said, "Yes," just as Bud said, "No."

"Right then," said their server. "One side of gravy comin' up."

Bud began scooping up scrambled eggs like she hadn't eaten in days. They clearly met with her approval, but she didn't begin to make yummy noises until she started on the bacon. She ate the three pieces provided in record time and then looked over at Cann's.

He snorted and pushed his plate closer. "Go ahead," he said. He motioned to the waitress and when she came over he said, "Bring us another order of bacon and make us two BLTs to go."

"Yep," she said and hurried off to the kitchen.

Bud smiled when she realized he was offering her all three pieces of his bacon. After snatching all of them, she bit into the first one with relish. He watched her mouth and cursed himself for the thought that came to mind. She was a kid.

"This is good," she said.

"Figured as much."

They ate in silence, paid the bill, and attracted just as much attention on the way out as they had on the way in. Not much exciting happens in small Texas panhandle towns. So little, in fact, that two people who were not locals eating at the café was news.

Out on the sidewalk, with a toothpick between his teeth, Cann said, "There's a People's Bank there on the corner. Why don't you walk over there with me?"

Bud pulled her bag tighter and looked up and down the street like she was weighing her options.

"Okay," she said.

The bank had only been open five minutes when they arrived. Cann walked up to the teller window.

"Need a blank check," he said.

"Do you have an account, sir?" asked the woman behind the glass.

"I do."

She placed a blank check and a pen in the little curved valley of a tray below the glass. Cann made it out for five hundred dollars then placed the check and the pen back in the tray.

"May I see your driver's license and your debit card?"

He pulled his wallet out of his pants, fished out the two plastic rectangles and placed them in the tray.

After performing several tasks that involved her keyboard, the teller said, "How would you like that, sir?"

"Two hundreds. Four fifties. Four twenties. Two tens."

"Just a minute, sir," she said. "I need to get your fifties from the back. Here's your ID."

She placed the two cards back into the tray.

Bud reached for his driver's license before he did and he made no move to stop her.

"Cannon Johns," she read from the face of his license. "Today's your birthday."

He hadn't remembered that and wouldn't have thought about it if she hadn't said something.

"Huh," he replied.

"My birthday is in another week."

"Huh," he repeated.

"This says you're only twenty-five. Today."

"Yeah. So?" He held his hand out for the license.

"You, ah, look older."

"Well." He sighed. "Not surprisin'."

The teller returned and said, "I'm going to count this out for you here." Cann nodded then watched her count the bills. "Would you like an envelope?"

"Yes. Thank you."

She put the money inside an envelope made for that purpose and set it in the tray.

Cann motioned for Bud to follow him to the counter where people stood to prepare transactions. They were still the only customers in the bank.

He took a fifty, two twenties, and a ten out of the envelope and put the cash in his wallet. He resealed the envelope and walked outside.

When they were on the sidewalk, he handed Bud the envelope.

Her eyes flew to his in surprise. "What's this?"

"It's money so you can rent your own bed tonight. I'll rest better knowin' you're gonna have somethin' to eat besides cheese crackers."

He shoved it toward her body and she took it out of reflex. "What I really want is a ride."

He'd already turned away from Bud and toward his bike. He stopped and turned around slowly. "Where?"

"Austin?"

"Look. Darlin'. I don't have to tell you that you're under age. You already know that. If it was next week, after your birthday, I'd give you a ride. Now? That's the kind of trouble I don't need."

"Please. I'm pregnant."

He froze for a couple of seconds before saying, "Jesus Christ. That is *really* the kind of trouble I don't need."

"What kind of trouble do you need?"

"You think this is a good time to be a smart ass?"

"It's not really a good time."

"Why are you out here in," he waved his arm, "this town?"

"My daddy wants me to have an abortion."

Cann looked skyward, ran a big hand through his hair and repeated, "Jesus Christ." He looked at her. "That's not legal, is it?"

"It's not legal to make me have an abortion, but if it's done privately, forcibly, it's his word against mine. And nobody's gonna believe me."

"What about your mother?"

"Died when I was five."

"Is this on the level?"

"Yeah."

"What are you gonna do when you get to Austin? You got any money besides the money I gave you?"

"Two dollars."

"You got relatives who'll help you?"

"Nobody."

"Jesus Christ. You got job skills?"

"Not as such."

"What does that mean?"

"Means I could work. I just haven't yet."

"High school?"

"Yeah. Graduated early." When he stared at her, she said, "I'm good at school."

"What about the…" he gestured toward her midsection, "father?"

She sneered. "He agrees with my daddy. Left to join the armed services. Don't know which one. Don't care. It's not like I loved him."

"Not like you loved him," Cann said.

His mind immediately went back to a day when he wasn't much older than Bud. The love of his life was standing in front of him looking worried about his reaction.

"I'm pregnant," she'd said.

It took a few seconds for that to sink in, but when it did, he grabbed her up and spun round and round. He laughed. She giggled. Until they fell down in the grass and lay looking into each other's eyes, making big plans for the future.

He knew he could take care of her and their baby even though he was too young to be starting a family by most people's estimation. He'd already decided what he was going to do and had been doing the groundwork. He had plans to combine his internet skills with his love of vintage muscle cars. He was going to start a nationwide business matching available parts with people who needed them.

It had worked.

He wasn't a billionaire, but he was making enough to take care of Molly and their little girl. He'd bought a stone house near Dripping Springs and the Sons of Sanctuary MC.

And life was good.

Until the day Molly hadn't been able to start her car. She needed corn meal for catfish and thought to take Cannon's truck instead. She moved the car seat, fastened the baby in, started the car and it had exploded. The car next to it, the one that wouldn't start, exploded as well. The house caught on fire and, by the time Cann knew about it, there was nothing left but ash and a few standing stones.

HE'D ALWAYS BEEN sure it was club related. Cann's

contribution to the club was mostly financial. They gave his business back office and warehouse support and he gave them a fair percentage. He belonged to Sons of Sanctuary because it was the kind of close knit, tribal community that everybody longs for. They would take care of his family if he couldn't. They'd take care of his business if he couldn't. And he'd do the same for them.

Cann had always supposed that whoever planted the explosives had mistaken his club function. In other words, they got him confused with somebody else. On a personal basis, he had no enemies.

His Molly. He worshiped her. They'd been together since they were fifteen and when he looked into the future, he only saw her face. Imagining life without her was impossible. The day his Molly died with their little girl he'd descended into hell and had been there ever since.

Most people who took the time to look in his face turned away feeling grateful that they were not that guy. It had been almost four years since he'd gone nomad. Every minute was a dull ache he couldn't escape. Every mile brought more emptiness until he couldn't really see the point of living at all.

Brant gave his permission and blessing when Cann asked to go NOMAD. Cannon Johns had changed the designation on his bottom rocker to NOMAD and taken to the road. Brant had told him that he was welcome back any hour of any day of forever.

Years later, Cann realized that demons couldn't be

outrun. They always kept pace. He wasn't ever going to outrun the pain. He wasn't ever going to outlive the pain. So he was going home to say goodbye to his friends and end it once and for all.

BUD HAD WATCHED in fascination as Cann's eyes glazed over. His thoughts had clearly taken him somewhere else.

He blinked twice and focused on the girl. "So you didn't love each other. Maybe that's a sweet mercy," he said in a rough voice.

"Maybe."

"So why do you want to keep the baby so much?"

She shrugged. "It's not the baby's fault that the sperm donor is an idiot."

"Yeah," he agreed. "Guess not. Why does your dad feel so strong about it?"

"He says it's cause he had plans for me. College. Blah. Blah. Blah. But the truth is that he thinks teenage pregnancy is trashy and he doesn't want people to know."

"What kind of people? Friends?"

"People he works with. My daddy doesn't really have what you'd call friends, I don't think."

Cann took in a big breath and let it out slowly. "So you're asking me to take you to Austin and what?"

"Just a ride. That's all. I'll find a job and never bother you. Swear."

"Uh-huh. You really want that baby?"

"Made up my mind."

"You know how hard it is to take care of a baby?"

She cocked her head. "You got kids?"

"I used to. Babies… it's not like getting a puppy. You have to be prepared to give them everything. Twenty-four hours a day. Whatever dreams you might have, they'll take a backseat, because the only thing that's important is the kid. You understand what I'm saying?"

"You a biker or a counselor?"

"Are you a smart ass or a girl who needs help?"

She shifted her weight to one leg and her shoulders sagged a little. "Girl who needs help."

"You got a driver's license?"

"Yes." To her credit, she answered without hesitation then stood waiting, perhaps hopefully, for what he would say next.

"Show it to me."

She unzipped the bag that was either a giant purse or a small overnighter and withdrew a red wallet. She fumbled a little trying to get the license free of its holder and Cann thought her hand might be shaking a little.

"Bud Slaughter McIntyre," he read out loud. Without lifting his chin, his eyes came up to meet hers. "You weren't lyin' about bein' named Bud." She shook her head. "Weren't lyin' about your birthday either." He looked down at the license in his hand. "You're from El Paso."

"Lately."

"What's that mean?"

"Means we move around every few years." She shrugged. "Daddy's job."

"No brothers or sisters?" She shook her head. "Grandparents? Aunts? Uncles?"

"I have grandparents, but I don't know them. They're strangers. So I wouldn't ask them for help." She trailed off as she realized that she'd just asked the stranger in front of her for help.

He smirked as he handed the license back. "I'll give you a ride if you promise you'll give your grandparents a call when you get to Austin. They might surprise you."

CHAPTER THREE

IN LESS THAN an hour they were on the outskirts of Amarillo, but dark clouds were gathering overhead. Cannon pulled off and looked at a weather radar app. He looked up directions to the nearest Chevy dealership and headed straight there.

When they pulled in, she said, "Why are we here?"

"Stayin' out of the rain, sugar."

Cannon pulled out a credit card and bought a three-year-old cargo van. He had them take the seats out and mount a ramp so he could get his bike inside. After they'd secured the motorcycle so that it wouldn't tip over, no matter what, they climbed into the cab and drove away.

"That's a lot of money to protect your bike from rain," she said.

"It's not the bike I'm trying to keep dry."

She looked out the window when she took his meaning. She didn't want to get attached to the big gruff biker, but knowing that he'd gone to such trouble and expense to take care of her left her heart lodged in her throat.

"If we do drive-through, eat in the car, we'll be there by seven tonight."

She said, "Okay," but her mind was racing. She had four hundred and two dollars to last until she could find a job and get paid. She couldn't figure out what the next step might be until she got where she was going and looked at the options one hour at a time. The only thing she knew for sure was that she couldn't let her father find her until she turned eighteen.

SHE WOKE UP to find that they were pulling into a fast food drive-through lane.

"Last Burger King you're gonna see for a while. What'll you have?" Cann said.

"Um, big fish sandwich. And a coke."

"No."

"No? What do you mean, no?"

"Nobody eats big fish sandwiches. It's a rule. This is not Fish King. It's *Burger* King."

"The baby likes fish."

He raised an eyebrow. "That's the story you're goin' with?"

She smiled. "Will that work?"

Cann turned back to the lighted menu board. "Yeah. That'll work."

When the voice prompted Cann to order, he rolled down his window and yelled at the microphone. "Double Whopper with cheese, a big fish sandwich, two large onion rings…" To Bud, he said, "You want French fries?" She nodded. "A regular fry, small coke and a bottled water." He looked at Bud then turned back to the mic.

"Cancel that coke order and make it two bottled waters."

"Hey," Bud said.

"You don't need all that sugar when you're pregnant."

She pretended to pout, but secretly loved that he cared whether she was taking care of herself and the baby, or not.

"I need to go to the bathroom," she said.

"Okay. You hop out and run around to the other side of the building. I'll get the food and pick you up over there."

He watched as she turned the corner and jogged out of sight.

After shoving cash through the window, Cann stowed the piping hot sack on the console and set the water bottles in the two drink holders, and drove around to the pedestrian entrance on the opposite side. He parked close to the door and left the car running, but only had to wait a couple of minutes before she was swinging back up into the van.

"That smells so good." She smiled.

As he backed out, he said, "You sort out who gets what while I get us back on the road."

"Again."

"What?"

"On the road again. You can't just say on the road. You have to say on the road *again*."

"Is that a rule?"

"Yes. It's in the same book that says nobody eats fish sandwiches."

"You really are a smart ass. Give me an onion ring."

"You're gonna smell like onions."

He chuckled. "You care?"

She shook her head. "No. I don't care."

"So your pop wanted you to go to college?"

"Yeah."

"Was he gonna pay for it?"

"Never asked him."

"What were you gonna study?"

"Not tellin'."

"Why?"

"'Cause you'd laugh."

Cann drove in silence for a couple of miles before saying, "Hog calling."

"What?"

"Since you're not telling me, I'm gonna guess. I'm thinking of things you might study that would cause somebody to laugh." She laughed. "So that's it?"

"No. That's not it."

"Underwear engineering."

"You know that's not a field of study. Right?"

"Somebody has to figure out how to make it fit. Right?"

"Yes. But I don't think they go to school for that. They just do trial and error until it's right."

"Okay. You name ten things a person such as yourself might go to college to learn and I'll guess which one you're interested in."

She contemplated that while finishing her bite of fish

sandwich. "Alright. Ten things. Astronomy. Medieval literature. Mandarin Chinese. City planning. Special education. Psychology. Computer programming. Theater. Architecture. Zoology." She picked up a couple of French fries and said, "Go," before putting them in her mouth.

"I get three guesses."

"Do not."

"It's my game. I get three guesses."

"It's my life. You do not."

"So you're saying I have to nail it on the first try or I'll never know?"

"Never say never, Johns."

"Sage advice. It's not Medieval literature or Mandarin Chinese or special education."

"Why not?"

"Because you added details to throw me off. If it was one of those things you would have just said literature, Chinese, or education."

"Huh."

He smiled inwardly, knowing that response meant he was right. "So that leaves seven. There's nothing laughable about computer programming or architecture or astronomy. So that leaves four possibilities. Zoology. That might be funny. Theater. Definitely funny. Psychology. A lot of people, including me, think that's funny. But I'm going to guess city planning."

She gasped. "How did you do that? Are you like psychic or something?"

He smiled. "Just worked it out logically."

"No. No. No." She was shaking her head. "You didn't just work it out logically. There's more to it than that."

He glanced out the window. "I've been on the road for a long time. Mostly alone. Lots of people-watching. I guess I picked up some instincts."

"Instincts."

"Yes. My instincts about you say city planning."

"Why?"

"Well, for one thing, being seventeen and completely without support or resources, but determined to keep a baby the dad doesn't want? That means you're optimistic about the future. I think city planners need to be optimistic about the future."

"Wow." She put the rest of her sandwich in the sack and settled back with the French fries. "So why have you been on the road? Alone?"

"Long story. Maybe another time. You want to drive for a while?"

"Um. Sure?"

"You do know how to drive, right? Otherwise, you wouldn't have a license."

"I do. I really do. I've just never driven on the highway."

Cann slowed down and pulled over. "Well, little mama, it's high time you did."

Five minutes later, Bud's seat and mirrors were adjusted and she was pulling back on the highway.

The two-lane State road between Lubbock and

Sweetwater wasn't heavily traveled. An occasional pickup truck or tractor were the only interruptions to a fairly constant landscape.

"You can go faster than forty?"

"You sure?" she asked.

He snorted softly. "You've really never driven a car faster than this?"

"First time," she affirmed.

"Well, at this pace, we're not gettin' to Austin until tomorrow."

She took a deep breath. "You're taking our lives into my own hands."

"You ever play video games?"

"Yeah. Sure."

"Then I'm not worried. Just gradually increase your speed until you feel comfortable goin' faster."

"K boss."

He left her alone to concentrate on driving for a while, but when it seemed that she had relaxed into road trip mode, he said, "So why did you think I'd laugh about city planning?"

She wagged her head from side to side. "Because it sounds high and mighty, I guess."

He didn't say anything for a few minutes. "All dreams sound high and mighty when there's a big distance between where you are and where you want to go." She smiled. "What?"

"You're a biker philosopher."

"Not really."

"What are you really?"

"This and that."

"What does that mean, Johns?"

He sighed. "I used to have a business. Online. I was a matchmaker."

"Shut up."

"Not that kind. I matched up vintage auto parts with people who were lookin' for 'em."

"Oh. What happened?"

"Walked out. I think it's still goin' on though." He laughed softly. "Business is probably gonna outlast me." He gave the landscape a rueful smile. "So. How does a girl from El Paso get interested in city planning?"

"That's the part where you'll laugh."

"Oh *that's* the part."

"Promise you won't laugh."

"Not gonna promise that, but I'll say this. If you can get a laugh outta me, you should get a prize for it."

"Why? Nothing is funny to you?"

"Spill it."

"Okay! Your license says you're twenty-five. Happy birthday, by the way. But you act like an *old* man."

"I *am* an old man who's not interested in birthdays. You gonna tell me or not?"

"Yes. I'm gonna tell you because there's nothing else to do in this car and I think you're right. Nothing I say is gonna make you laugh."

"It's a van. Not a car. And I think you should go into sales. You can talk around somethin' without sayin' what you mean more than anybody I've ever met."

"Huh."

He laughed.

"You laughed!" she said.

"All right. You get the prize."

"Look. I'm going sixty-five."

"Tryin' to keep my heartrate steady."

"Well, speed may not be new to you…"

"Stop right there. This, what we're doing here, is *not* speed."

"You're just saying that because you're not driving."

"That makes no sense."

"Whatever."

"City planning."

"SimCity." He shook his head. "That doesn't mean anything to you?"

"No. Should it?"

"Well, yeah! You never saw the Sim games?"

"No."

"Well, this guy who knew my dad from work gave us some of these computer games. You can build virtual cities, but you have to take all the details into account, like commercial zones, residential zones, where to put the streets and parks, what the buildings should look like and what their functions are. You have to figure out quality of life. Where people work in relationship to where they live and where they play. Where should schools go? Where should water treatment go? What about garbage? And you have a budget you have to work with.

"Then later there were all these other editions like SimCity Amusement Park. That one was *really* fun." She laughed. "It even had a little guy who yakked after he got off the roller coaster. It was hysterical." Cann looked at her like she'd lost her mind. "Oh and SimCity of the Future.

"I loved those games. I could spend a whole weekend fooling around with this and that, trying to make it perfect, and I never got tired of it."

"But that's not the way cities get built in real life."

"I know. But…"

"But what?"

"Modern cities are reconceiving themselves. They're hiring people to figure out how to repurpose or renew to keep the population closer to where they work and play. That's way more challenging than building a virtual city from the ground up. And way more exciting because it's real people and real lives."

Cann took over the driving after a restroom stop, but Bud continued to talk about the ins and outs of city planning until they stopped at a barbeque buffet in Abilene, but took the food to go.

When they were back in the car with brisket sandwiches, she said, "So Austin is home?"

"Yeah. I haven't been back for a while, but I was born there."

Since they were only three hours away, he thought it would be a good time to figure out what he was going to do with her when they got there.

"You thought about where you want me to drop you?"

"Yeah," she said. "Since you know the town and all, I thought you could recommend a semi-safe neighborhood with a good walk score."

"What the hell is a walk score?"

"It means it's a place where you can live without a car. You can walk to work and get groceries and stuff like that."

He harrumphed, which did serve to support his claim that he was an old man in a young man's body. "Look. I don't have to tell you this ain't New York. The only place that has a good 'walk score' is the University of Texas and I'm tellin' you right now you can't afford to live around there."

Her shoulders sagged as she slumped back against the front passenger seat. "Bus score?"

He snorted and shook his head. "Last time I was home, we had some junkers out back at Rides and Wrecks. Maybe we can find you somethin' that runs. And you can pay us back when you're a famous city planner."

She turned to look at Cann in the gathering twilight. She felt emotion pressing behind her eyes and felt tears trying to form. She took in a deep breath and determined she wouldn't cry.

"You're an awful nice man, Johns. You gave me money. For no reason. Now you're saying you might find me a car and let me pay it out? I'm not so unlucky, 'cause you're the one who found me."

Cann was on the verge of being embarrassed. He didn't feel like a nice man. He felt like a wretched man.

"Now just stop that business right now. Everybody needs a hand up now and then. It's no big deal."

"It is a big deal." He waved her off by spreading the fingers on the hand that gripped the steering wheel. "What is Rides and Wrecks?"

"It's an outfit my club owns. Makes custom vehicles for celebrities and rich people who need shiny toys."

"Sons of Sanctuary?"

"Yeah."

"What does nomad mean?"

Cann didn't answer for a few minutes. "It means you got no home."

"But I thought you were going home?"

"I am."

"So you're not going to be nomad anymore?"

"That's right. I'm done." He was done with being nomad and he was done talking about the subject. "Now about tonight. I can take you to a motel if you want to dive into some of that cash you've got in that thing you carry. But we've got a guest room at the club where you could stay if you want. Just for tonight. Nobody will bother you. Tomorrow morning we can fix you up with a ride and maybe you can find a job." He looked for the headlights since they hadn't come on automatically. "And a doctor."

"A doctor."

"Remember when I told you babies are work?" She

nodded. "It starts now. You have to take vitamins and eat good and go to appointments to make sure everything is okay."

"Okay," she said softly, touched that he actually seemed to care what happened to a stranger and her baby.

IT WAS AROUND eight when they blew past the Austin city limits. Just before they reached the club compound, he realized that, for the first time in years, he'd spent several hours awake and not sad. But that revelation didn't bring him either relief or satisfaction. It made him feel guilty, like he'd deliberately betrayed the memory of Molly and the baby.

When he pulled up to the SSMC gate, a voice on the box said, "Cann. That you?"

"Yeah, it's me. Let me in."

A kid came trotting over to open the gate. After they parked, Bud got her bag and followed Cann inside. What happened next was hardly the kind of homecoming he'd imagined.

There on the giant screen TV was a freeze-frame image of him with Bud at the bank in Barburnett. Several club members including Brant and Brash were standing and sitting around the bar, looking unhappy to say the least.

When Cann saw the image, he froze in his tracks and gaped. "What the…"

"You're a wanted man," said Brant with alarming

calm. "Everybody's looking for that little girl. After her picture had been plastered on the news, the bank at Barburnett called in a report that she was in the bank, probably under duress, with a shady character who's a member of a motorcycle 'gang'."

Brant practically spit that word. He hated having his club referred to as a gang.

"Needless to say," Brant continued, "you will not be staying long. But we'd like to enjoy your company long enough to find out what the fuck is going on."

Cann turned to Bud. "Do you know anything about this?"

His stomach roiled when he saw that she looked sheepish. "My daddy may be abusing his office some."

"His office? What does that mean?" Cann practically boomed.

Bud took a tentative step back and looked around the room anxiously. "He's a Texas Ranger?"

"Jesus Christ!" Cann turned his back on her, ran a hand through his hair, and pulled on it in a way that looked painful. "You've brought the Rangers here?"

She shook her head. "I didn't. I just got a ride."

"To the Ranger capital of the world?!?" He was full-on shouting.

"How'd you end up with this girl, Cann?" Brant interrupted what was building up to a full-on tirade.

"She's pregnant and a week shy of eighteen. Says her daddy was gonna force her to get rid of it. She's tryin' to avoid him until her birthday."

Brant shook his head, but looking around the room he could tell that any one of them, in the same circumstance, might have done the same thing.

"Just a week?" Brant directed the question to Bud. She nodded solemnly, looking a little scared. "You healthy?" She looked confused by the question, but nodded again.

"Where's your bike?" Brant asked Cann.

"Inside the van."

"Where'd you get the van?"

"Bought it used in Amarillo at a Chevy dealership."

"Why?"

"Looked like rain." It was Cann's turn to look sheepish. Axel and Burn, who were sitting at the bar, turned away but didn't do a very good job of hiding their laughter.

"Well," Brant said, "chances are the folks at Chevy saw you, too." He glanced at Bud. "So here's what you're gonna do. You're gonna take Arnold's new dually that still has paper plates on it and go out to the safe house in Big Bend. It has spare tanks so you won't have to stop for gas. Go shave that beard off and cut your hair so you won't be recognized. Do not wear your cut."

To Bud he said, "If you gotta go, you're gonna have to go by the side of the road."

She stared at Brant, too scared of him to say anything.

Turning back to Cann, he continued. "Take enough provisions so you don't have to leave that house until she's eighteen goddamn years old. Am I understood?"

"Jesus Christ," said Cann.

"What was that?"

"Yeah, boss," Cann corrected.

"Good. While you're making yourself look like a nice clean-cut tradesman, we'll be loading the truck."

"You hungry?" he asked Bud. She shook her head vigorously. "You worth all this trouble?" She stared at Brant for a few beats and then grinned. "You got somethin' to say to me?"

"Thank you?" she said.

"If we all get out of this," he pointed toward her belly, "him or her included, without charges being filed, you can name him or her after me."

"No promises," she said.

Brant looked at Cann. "World of shit, brother." Cann was wearing an expression that said he agreed completely. "Oh," Brant chuckled, "there's no electricity at the safe house. There were some old dusty books last time I was there, but it's been a long time."

To the room in general Brant said, "Come on everybody. Hop to. We've got to get them on their way outta here before the Rangers track Cann to us." He looked at Cannon pointedly. "Which will be any minute. Give me the keys to the van."

When Cann handed them over, Brant threw the keys to Burn. "You and Axel get that thing outta here and make sure it isn't found."

"My bike's in there. And my stuff," Cann told Burn.

"They're not lookin' for the bike. Park it in plain sight and stow his stuff in the dually. Give me your phone."

Brant passed the phone on to Axel. "For Christ's sake, get that out of here, too."

Brant turned to Bud and she had to resist the impulse to step behind Cann's body for cover. "You got a phone, young lady?" She shook her head no, looking a little wide-eyed that she was being addressed directly by the guy who was apparently king of all he surveyed.

"She tellin' the truth?" he asked Cann.

Cann looked down at Bud. "Truthfully, I don't know."

Bud narrowed her eyes at Cann like he was a traitor, but her more logical half agreed that he had no way of knowing who she was, what she'd do, or why she'd do it.

She put her bag on the ground, unzipped it and left it open for them to look. Then she unzipped her jacket, held it out to the sides and turned around slowly.

That seemed to satisfy everybody because they turned to going about their assigned tasks.

Brash called his wife to come quick because she was pretty handy around a pair of scissors. She was there in ten minutes.

When Cannon walked out into the club's main room, Bud had to do a double take. He looked ten years younger without the beard and the cut. He was wearing a gray knit hoodie. But his youthful look was overshadowed by the menace of the glower he was wearing. She was having second thoughts about not mentioning her daddy's profession, but she really hadn't thought the old man would pull strings to make it look like she was a kidnap victim.

"All loaded," Brant said as they walked toward the dually. "Take the back way and don't poke your heads up until that girl is legal. Here's directions to the house." Cann took the map and printed directions. "We'll call the caretakers. There's a family close by that will tidy up, make sure the sheets are clean, stock firewood. This time of year might be cold at night. Might be hot as blazes durin' the day. They'll leave you some gallon-size bottles of water and bags of ice in coolers. Closest thing to a refrigerator. Maria'll stop by once a day to see if you need anything."

"Sorry to bring this down on y'all. I didn't know," said Cann.

"I know you didn't. Now get going. This ain't the old days. We're not lookin' for shootouts with Rangers. Speaking of that. There's some artillery in the floor compartment. Sometimes ther're hostiles in the badlands. Do not do anything to call attention to yourselves." Cann gave a tight nod and turned the engine over. "There's two thermoses of coffee there," he pointed to the thermal carrier, "'cause you're not sleepin' tonight. Stay away from the interstates. Head toward Uvalde and Del Rio. Take 90 out to Marfa and then drop down."

"I know how to avoid confrontations, Brant." Cann felt bad about bringing trouble to the MC doorstep, but he still had a modicum of self-respect.

Brant pressed on undeterred as was his right as the last word on what happened on SSMC grounds. "Yeah, well, you're not by yourself this time, are ya? House is so close to the river... if you see somebody comin' who looks suspicious, the two of you wade across and call me on this." He handed Cann a burner phone. "Rangers won't cross into Mexico." Brant lowered his voice. "But I'm tellin' you right now, do *not* touch that jail bait. Find a way to keep your wick soft for a week. There's no hot water out there. So it shouldn't be hard." Brant laughed when he caught his own accidental pun.

Cannon Johns gaped at the prez in utter astonishment, not finding him the least bit funny.

"Just sayin'." Brant chuckled softly. "And when you get back you and I are gonna have a real-McCoy-type sit down concerning your future. For now you take this." Brant handed over a fistful of cash. Five hundred dollars worth of U.S. currency. Five hundred dollars in fifty, one hundred, and two hundred peso notes.

Bud had been listening so intently, trying to overhear what was being said between Cann and the old guy she'd secretly named Billy Goat Gruff, she jumped when Brigid knocked on her window. She looked around for the button that would lower it.

"Hi." Brigid smiled. "There's not time to go shopping or gather stuff up for you, but here's what we had around the clubhouse. A few magazines."

"Thank you."

Bud's tone was so sincere that Brigid was struck by it. It made her wonder if small kindnesses had been rare in her young life.

CHAPTER FOUR

Cann turned away from town.

Bud said, "I'm sorry. I know this isn't the way you expected your homecoming to go."

"Yeah, well." He rested both hands at the top of the steering wheel. It didn't escape Bud's notice that the pose showcased his biceps. "Turns out it's a textbook case of no good deed shall go unpunished." He snorted derisively. "Happy birthday to me."

Bud let that comment hang heavy in the air of the truck cab for half an hour before saying, "Where are we going?"

"Just on the other side of Big Bend." Cann's anger was still palpable, but starting to wear off. "You been there?"

"Big Bend? No. We didn't, um, do vacations."

"Yeah? Well, it's wild. Remote. That's not all bad. One of the best things about it is that you can see the stars just like it was a thousand years ago. No light pollution in the night sky."

"Light pollution," she repeated quietly.

"I know what you're thinkin'."

"What?"

"That you can't plan cities without lights. You need 'em to drive by and keep people safe. All the advertising though? We could do without it."

"Commerce is what fuels modern life."

"So they say." He reached down and opened the air vents to let in some fresh air. "It's quiet, too. So quiet you can hear somebody comin' from a long ways off. I mean if it's an engine."

"I knew what you meant. You're not gonna get into trouble for this."

Cann snorted. "How do you figure that? If your daddy wants to claim I kidnapped a minor, he'll do it. And who do you think people are gonna believe? Me? Or a Texas Ranger?"

"They're not like almighty virtue, you know."

"Doesn't matter. Public perception is what matters. Once again. Who do you think people are gonna believe? Me? Or him?"

She stared hard at Cann's profile. "I think they'll believe me."

He barked out a derisive laugh. "Really? And what are you gonna tell 'em, little girl?"

"I'm not a little girl. When I get the chance, I'm gonna tell the truth. That you're this baby's hero. That he owes you his life. He or, um, she."

Cann could tell by her ragged intake of breath that she meant what she said. And for a second or two, it felt to Cann like time froze in place. The last thing that he'd ever expected to be called in this life or any other was *hero*.

Of course he knew Molly felt that way, but it was just a vague idea of loving him no matter what. Not the kind of thing the girl meant.

"I'm no hero. I'm just a guy who happened across a runaway girl."

"That's what makes you a hero, Johns. People come across runaways every day and just keep walkin'. Not you." She watched his profile illuminated by the dashboard lights and repeated, "You're different." He glanced out the driver's side window and almost missed what she said next because it was so quiet. "Special."

He didn't know what to think about that or feel about it either. Cann knew he wasn't the world's most educated guy, but if there was one thing he did know, it was that he was *not* special. Different, maybe.

After they'd ridden in silence for a while, Bud said, "You want me to pour you some coffee?"

Cann nodded. "Yeah. That'd be good."

"Are you sleepy?" she asked.

He smiled. "No. But I probably will be before we get there."

"You want me to drive?"

"I've seen the way you drive, sugar. You're not getting behind the wheel at night on the roads between here and Big Bend. We need to go as fast as we can without getting stopped and the two-lane blacktops have surprises at night."

"What kind of surprises?"

"Cows that get out. We'd definitely survive that in this dually, but we don't want to be left by the side of the road with a cow carcass and a disabled vehicle. Other animals wander out onto the road sometimes. Deer that…"

"Get caught in headlights?"

They both laughed.

"Yes. Sometimes signs are down right before you get to a hairpin curve. One time, way out near where we're goin', I saw twin mountain lions by the side of the road. Babies. Not more than a few months old. Damnedest thing."

"Mountain lions?" She sounded alarmed.

"Told you it's wild out there. And remote."

"But mountain lions?"

"They gotta live somewhere and they have no appreciation for city planning."

"Ha. Ha. Are there lots?"

"Lots of mountain lions?" He smiled wickedly. "At least two." She looked out into the darkness. "Not here. We just left Austin. Bet you can get somethin' on the radio."

She turned on the radio and scanned the dial from one end to the other then said, "That's it. What's your pleasure?"

"Don't care. You choose."

BUD PUT IT on a country station and settled back into the passenger seat.

Cann was thinking back to Molly's pregnancy and how awful morning sickness had been.

"You ever get sick?" he said. "At your stomach?"

"I did." Her hand automatically went to her abdomen like she couldn't talk about it without touching. "That's over now. It wasn't fun at all."

"So if you graduated from high school in June and your dad wanted you to go to college, how come you're not in school?"

"I was gonna go to Texas Tech, but I found out I was pregnant. So I told Daddy I decided I wanted to go to a different school and start in January. The different school part was true."

"Where was it you wanted to go?"

"Where does everybody in the known universe who's in their right mind want to go? The University of Texas, Austin."

He nodded. "Don't imagine Texas Tech has much to say about city planning."

"Tell me about it."

"So why were you goin' there?"

"Daddy was transferred to the Lubbock office last month."

"And you needed to go where he was living?"

"He wanted me to live at home. I guess so he wouldn't have to pay somebody else to do the stuff I do."

"What kind of stuff do you do?"

"You know. Everything. Shopping. Cleaning up. Laundry. Cooking."

"Seriously."

"Yeah. It's just been the two of us most of my life. When I was little he got help sometimes, but he told them to teach me how to do stuff and by the time I was, hmmm, maybe eleven? I could handle it."

"Jesus." Cann was remembering what he'd been doing when he was eleven. He and his brother had been out on bicycles looking for trouble and never failing to find it.

"What? It's not as bad as it sounds. Actually it was pretty good because he was gone a lot and I could do what I wanted."

"You mean he left you alone? When you were eleven?"

"Don't sound so shocked. I was very mature for my age."

"Like you are now."

"You teasing me, Johns?"

As that question seeped into his brain, his mind immediately formed a picture of Molly hanging sheets on a line to dry. Her grandmother had taught her that sheets dried in clean air have a smell and crisp feel that no dryer can reproduce. It was a lot of extra trouble, but Molly thought it was worth it.

So Cann had put a clothes line at the back of their property and once a week plain white sheets could be seen hanging from the parallel lines. He'd been surprised that

Target had wooden clothes pins. He would have thought they'd be a vintage item for sale on Ebay or some such, but there they were as she said they'd be. He bought enough to last a lifetime.

He'd come home one day in the middle of the afternoon and surprised her while she was hanging up the sheets. He grabbed her from behind and breathed in deep, as always enjoying the fruity smell of her shampoo. When she squealed, the baby who was sitting in the playpen nearby was startled and kicked up a fuss. It took some doing to convince his little girl that Cann was a good reliable daddy and not a monster.

All the while he was trying to calm the baby down, Molly was laughing at him for starting a ruckus.

She had a wide smile and a sunny disposition that seemed to fit her auburn hair and light freckles. He thought she was as beautiful as a goddess fallen to Earth.

"Johns?"

"Hmmm?"

"Where'd you go?"

"Right here." He replayed the question in his head and was shocked to realize that teasing was exactly what he'd been doing. Since when did he tease? "Why do you keep calling me Johns?"

"Same reason you call me sugar. You don't like Bud. I don't like Cannon."

His response was a grunt, but it was agreeable.

By midnight Cann had drunk half a thermos of coffee

and was ready for a roadside spray. Apparently he wasn't the only one thinking that.

"I have to go to the bathroom," Bud said.

"Okay. Side of the road is the best I can do."

"What?"

"Any place that has bathrooms has cameras and TVs. People have seen your face. You're a kidnapped child. I'm an outlaw. This is how it is."

"I'm not a child."

"I'm not an outlaw. Still. Here we are."

"I can't see snakes in the dark."

He sighed. "All right. I'll run the snakes off for you first."

"You can do that?"

He grinned at her. "How long did you say you've been in Texas?"

"All my life."

"If you say so."

They were well past Uvalde and, at that time of night, it was really unlikely that another car would come by. Cann eased off to the side of the road and parked. He walked around to her side of the truck, stomped around, yelled a little, then opened her door.

"There ya go. Snakes all gone. I'll go back around the other side so you can have some privacy."

She didn't like it, but couldn't argue that it was the only choice. She worked up the courage to walk a few feet away. Luckily there were a couple of tissues in the bottom of her bag. She squatted and was relieved to realize that pee doesn't make any sound when it hits the dirt. Feeling a lot less embarrassed, she walked back to the truck.

Cann had taken the opportunity to relieve himself on the other side of the road and was back at the truck by the time she got there.

"You good?" he said.

"Yeah. It was an adventure."

He snickered and started the engine. "That's really the first time you've ever peed in the great outdoors?"

"Yes. Men are made differently, you know."

"No," he said seriously, "I hadn't noticed that."

"So. Are you in a lot of trouble with your, ah, gang?"

Even in the dim light from the dashboard she could tell that he was giving her a withering look.

"It's not a gang. It's a club."

"Okay. Don't be so sensitive."

"It's not being *so* sensitive to want to get things right."

"Club. Gang. Who really cares, Johns?"

He turned on the radio and fooled with the dial. The only station he could get clearly was on AM, a bible thumper preaching God, guns, and gays. For the first two. Against the last.

"We're not really going to listen to this, are we?" she asked.

"Not a big range of options out here and I need to stay alert."

"*This* is gonna keep you alert?"

He smiled. "Not likely to get sleepy with that goin' on."

Cann was a little amazed that he was smiling, given the fact that he'd brought a heap of trouble right to the SSMC doorstep. Potentially. He reached over and shut off the radio abruptly.

"Why didn't you tell me?"

"That my daddy's a Ranger?" He gave her a glance that said no nonsense. "There was no reason to think it'd be an issue."

"Not an issue," he repeated drily.

"Look. He's gone for weeks at a time. That's how it's always been. How did I know he was gonna come home?"

"I don't know how you knew it, but you obviously did. That's why you ran, right? If you'd thought he was gonna stay away until after your birthday, you would've stayed in a nice warm, *dry* comfy place." He emphasized the word 'dry' to remind her that when they'd met she'd been in a situation that spelled desperate any way you looked at it.

Her shoulders sagged. "I didn't know when or if, Johns. Honestly. But I couldn't take that chance. When he left, he said, 'When I get back we'll be taking care of things'."

"So he's not getting a 'parent of the year' award."

She snorted. "He kept the water and lights and gas turned on. Left money for groceries and stuff. That was pretty much it."

"So you're sayin' you raised yourself?"

"Not exactly. I had a next door neighbor who kind of looked out for me. She taught me how to do stuff that men don't know how to do."

"Toenail paintin'?"

"No. Laundry."

He barked out a laugh. "You think men don't know how to do laundry?"

"I never met any."

"Sure you have."

"What're you saying? That you know how to do laundry?" He gave a quick dip of the chin. "You're lyin'."

"Whatever."

"Maybe you'll get a chance to prove it to me."

He laughed. "So you're sayin' that, if I play my cards right, I *might* get to do your laundry? Pretty slick, kid."

"How'd you learn to do laundry?"

Cann's good humor died a death as sudden as a balloon pricked by a pin.

Bud not only saw it. She felt it, too. The atmosphere in the cab of the truck became heavy, pregnant with something. Sorrow maybe.

"Tell me what happened, Johns." He said nothing, just stared ahead at the ribbon of blacktop illuminated solely by his own headlights. "I'm stumbling all over your landmines. If we're going to be together for a week, I need to know where they're located."

He sucked in a big breath suddenly, almost like he'd forgotten to breathe until his body went into survival and overrode his brain.

"It's not a kid story, sugar. It's a grown up story."

"You got away with that I'm-so-much-older-than-you thing when you were hidin' under that big red beard, but I can see your face now. You're not that much older than me." He opened his mouth to speak, but she cut him off. "I can see you're gearin' up to repeat the whole I'm-an-old-man-in-a-young-man's-body thing. I may not have the same experiences as you, but I've been taking care of myself and running a household for most of my life. Not hanging out at the mall. That doesn't make me ancient, but it does mean I'm responsible."

He glanced over at his passenger and noticed her fingertips were lightly petting her belly, like she was trying to soothe the tiny person growing inside her.

Christ, he thought. *Life really is a miracle.*

"Okay. I hear you. I'll make a deal. It's not a pretty story. Hell to live. Hell to tell. I'll tell you what happened. You can ask questions if you want, but only until we get to the safe house. That's my deal. After that, I don't ever want to hear anything about it again."

"Okay," she said quietly.

"I had a girl. Her name was Molly. She was just like her name sounds. Pretty. Optimistic. Good heart through and through. Met her when I was fifteen and that was it for me. Pretty soon after high school she turned up pregnant. I can't say I was sorry. I was too busy bein' happy to be sorry.

"I had a little business that was taking off. I told you about it before. Matchmaking. Online parts." Bud nodded. "We got married and, by the time the baby came, I had enough money to make a down payment on a house. She picked it out. Austin stone is what they call it. It wasn't huge, but we didn't have a big family. Just Molly, me and the baby."

Cann stopped talking for a while. Bud supposed he'd gotten lost in thought, like mentally turning through the pages of a photo album located in his memories.

"Boy or girl?" Bud gently prompted to get him to come back to the conversation.

"Girl. Kiley Marie."

"Pretty name."

"Yeah. Molly and I both had reddish hair. Kiley's was flaming." He chuckled. "Eyes so big and blue I used to say she looked like a cartoon.

"I had a pickup I used for bad weather days. Molly never drove it, but maybe her car didn't start. She got in the truck and it was rigged with explosives that…" When Cann didn't finish the sentence, Bud knew he was trying to steady his voice. "It was meant for me. Both cars blew. House caught fire."

Bud looked out the passenger window feeling a little bit sick at her stomach and wishing she hadn't pressed him to tell her. "Oh God."

It had been a couple of hours since the last time they'd seen another car. He looked at his watch. "We'll be there in an hour. After that, you're never gonna mention this again."

"That's why you've been… nomad." He nodded.

"Why were you coming back now?"

That was the one question he hadn't expected her to

ask. And it was the one question he wasn't prepared to answer. At least not fully.

"I wanted to take care of some business."

"And then what?"

She wasn't going to let it go as easily as he'd hoped.

"I've told you everything pertinent. The rest is my business."

"Pertinent?"

"Yes, *Bud*. Pertinent."

"Don't you *Bud* me!"

He smirked. "That *is* your name. Right?"

"Yes. It is. *Sugar*."

His smirk grew. If that was supposed to be a dig, it had the opposite effect. He kind of liked it when she called him 'sugar'. He kind of liked it when she called him 'Johns', too.

They rode in silence for a while without even the middle of the night fire and brimstone preachers to distract each of them from their private thoughts.

"There's a little more coffee," Bud said quietly. "You want it?"

He nodded.

When she handed him the thermos lid that doubled as a cup, he took it gratefully. Bringing it to his lips, he felt the steam rise and settle on his face. An involuntary sigh caused his chest to rise and fall.

Bud wasn't going to offer condolences. She sensed he'd take it as empty words, hollowed out all the more by all the time that had passed. But that didn't mean that she didn't feel the pain in his voice. It didn't mean that she wasn't sympathetic. She couldn't imagine having that kind of happiness, people to love who love you back, and having it destroyed so suddenly and in such a grotesque manner.

The fact that he was sure it was a murder meant for him made the whole of it simply unbearable. And she marveled that he'd held himself together at all.

No, she wasn't going to tell him she was sorry, because that wasn't what he needed from her, but she hoped that somehow he knew it.

"Are you sure it wasn't some kind of freak accident?"

"Yeah."

"Are you sure it was meant for you?"

"Yeah."

"Did you uh… find out who did it?"

He turned his head away for a second, glancing out the driver's side window at the darkness. When he looked at the road again, he said, "No."

It was one of the shortest, most concise words in the English language, but it was infused with so much feeling, mostly bitter resentment, that it conveyed paragraphs of information.

"Have you thought about what you'd do if you found out?"

He hesitated for just a second before saying, "Every damn second of every damn day." He pulled out the phone Brant had given him. "You know how to use the flashlight app on this phone?"

She took the phone. "Of course. I didn't just crawl out from under a rock."

He let that go. "All right. I need you to help us find the place. Look right there on top in the console and get that paper. Then read me what it says. I think we're gettin' close to the turn off."

"You can't put it in GPS?"

"There's no addresses out here, sugar."

"Oh."

CHAPTER FIVE

"Stayin' at the club tonight," Brant told Garland.

"Why?" she asked.

"We might be gettin' a visit from the Texas Rangers. If we do, I need to be here to control the message."

She laughed. "You mean you don't trust Burn to be spokesperson for the club?"

"Thanks for the cold shiver that just ran up my back."

She laughed again. "Okay then. I'm watching telenovelas."

"Good. Get the crap out of your system while I'm not there."

"It's not crap. Alejandro is about to find out that Miranda is really his daughter."

"Christ. Don't forget to set the alarm."

"Who needs an alarm with these dogs, Brant? I feel sorry for the poor ne'er-do-well that tries to come in here uninvited."

"Just set the alarm."

"Okay."

"I mean it, Garland."

"Okay! I will."

BRANT HAD BARELY hung up when Arnold said, "At the gates, boss."

Brant had a choice to make. He could walk out beyond the gate and talk with whoever'd been sent and he'd be perfectly within his rights to keep the law at a distance. But going out of his way to seem open to inspection might dispel a cause for warrants. If he could lay suspicion to rest and send the dogs off in a different direction, that would be a win. Definitely the smarter choice.

For years the club had been squeaky clean when it came to such things as drugs. After all, Brant had raised a child there.

"Tell Juice to send 'em on up."

ARNOLD LOOKED SURPRISED, but nodded.

Brant walked out into the main room. "Shut that off." He motioned to the TV as he barked the order at the prospect behind the bar. Everybody gave Brant their immediate and undivided attention. "Rangers on the way up. Just relax. If they ask if you've seen Cann, the answer is…"

In unison everybody in the room said, "No."

Brant nodded his satisfaction with that. He looked up at the security cameras that simultaneously showed six views of the compound and grounds. "Shut that down and make sure the feed from the past two days is destroyed. Now!"

Rally hurried toward the server room to make sure the cameras were offline. They went dark just as Arnold was opening the door for the Rangers.

"Welcome, gentlemen," Arnold said.

Two armed Rangers stepped inside. The first was Forge Russell, whom Brant had known most of his life. The Fornight family had always had ties to the Rangers. In fact the founder was a great-uncle of Brant's, and one of his dad's brothers had served.

Brant came forward and stuck out his hand. "Russ," he said. "What brings you out here?"

"Brant. Got a situation." The guy next to Russell was young enough to be his kid. Brant guessed he was a new partner. "This is R.W. Mackey." After Brant shook hands with the younger man, Russell said, "We don't want to disturb your evenin'. Just have a couple of questions. Got some place where we can talk?"

Brant looked around. There were twenty-odd people in the room. "Oh." Brant played ignorant. "You mean some place where everybody doesn't hear what you got to say?"

Russell almost rolled his eyes, but leveled on Brant and his defiant smirk instead. "Yes," he said evenly. "That is what I mean."

"You can come on back to the office, but it's kind of tight in there."

"That's okay. We won't be long."

"Suit yourself."

THE TWO RANGERS followed Brant back to the office, the younger one doing his best to visually record every detail and not miss a thing.

Brant sat down behind his messy desk and motioned for the two other men to sit in the two old wood deacon's chairs. Russell sat, but Mackey chose to stand by the closed door.

Brant waited patiently.

"Seems we're lookin' for one of your boys," Russell said.

"Oh?"

"Yeah."

"Well. I'm guessin' it's not for a speedin' ticket, since that's outside the purview of Ranger business."

"Now, Brant. You know perfectly well that Ranger business is whatever we decide to make it."

"State your business, Russ. I have a telenovela to watch with my wife."

Russell chuckled softly. "I'd almost like to see that. I really would. But tonight I'm lookin' for an SSMC member, wanted for kidnapping. For starters."

Brant shook his head. "Kidnapping," he said drily. "Now, Russ. You know good and well that none of my boys are gonna be kidnappin' anybody. That's not just ridiculous. It's ludicrous. And you know it."

"I'm finding it kind of interesting that you're not askin' who it is we're lookin' for."

"I know who you're lookin' for, Russ. We have a TV."

"Well, sure." Russ smiled. "That explains that."

"I also know that Cannon Johns is not a kidnapper. I strongly suspect you know that, too."

"Maybe I do. Thing is," he paused to make a face that looked more like a wince than anything, "girl's pop is one of us."

"Like I said. Got a TV out there. Big one, too."

Russell nodded while clearly assessing Brant for truth telling. "Course you'd tell me if you'd seen him."

"You'd be the first one I'd call."

"Yeah. That's what I thought." Russell smiled. "Could we maybe have a look at your internal camera feed? Just in case he came in and out without you noticin'?"

"Well, sure. Let's go on out here. We'll all watch it together. Maybe make popcorn."

"That's very nice of you, Brant. I hurried over here without dinner."

BACK IN THE main room, Brant said, "Rally? Ranger Russell here would like to see our video for the last couple of days."

Rally shook his head. "Sorry, boss. We've been down since Tuesday."

"Oh? I didn't know that," Brand said. Turning to Russell, he said, "Sorry about that. I didn't know."

Russell nodded. "Shame about the popcorn."

"Yep. There's a cantina over in Dripping Springs."

"Yeah. I know it. You mind if I ask the rest of these folks if they've seen our man?"

"Be my guest," Brant said.

"For the record," Russell addressed the entire room, "have any of you seen Cannon Johns recently?"

Everybody shook their head no except for Brash, who said, "Not except on TV."

Russ looked Brash over. "This one yours?"

Brant looked at Brash like he was trying to decide. "Yeah. He's one of 'em."

"You got two?" Russell seemed surprised.

"Long story," Brant said.

"Well, maybe another time."

"Yep."

RALLY ALREADY HAD the camera feed up and running again by the time Juice closed the gate after the Rangers.

CHAPTER SIX

Driving slow, reading from Brant's typed note with headlights on bright, they found the dirt road turn off.

"It's kind of… I don't know," she said.

"Remote? Dark? Barren?"

"Yes. I guess it's all those things. Maybe it'll look different in the light?" His only answer was a brief bark of laughter. "This says, 'The gas isn't turned on. So if you want hot water, you'll have to heat it on the fireplace. If you want hot food, you'll have to cook it on the fireplace'." She looked at Cann. "Are. You. Serious?"

He shrugged. "Good thing it's turned cool then."

When the headlights hit the rock exterior of the house, Bud said, "That's it?"

"I'm guessin' so."

The entire place appeared to be no bigger than twenty-two feet square, but there was a ramshackle detached garage. When he saw it, Cann saw the wisdom in that. A safe house isn't safe if a vehicle is parked outside saying, "I'm here. Come and get me."

When they pulled up next to the house and stopped

the truck, Bud seemed hesitant to get out.

"What's the matter?" Cann asked.

"I don't know. It's just so…"

"Listen, darlin'. You want to keep that baby safe. This is what safe means."

"You know that for a fact? That we're safe here?"

Years ago he'd come to believe that the *only* thing he knew for a fact was that he would not ever allow himself to love anyone again.

"I think so. But it's the best option we've got. Right?"

"Right," she said. "And you forgot. I'm sugar. Not darlin'."

"I *forgot*?" He smirked. "What's the difference?"

"Darlin' is biker speak for all women under sixty who are something less than butt ugly."

He felt a full-throated laugh bubble up before he could tamp it down. Damn if she wasn't right. He'd never given much thought to when and how the term was used, but she'd pretty much nailed it.

"According to your imaginary lexicon, what does 'sugar' mean in 'biker speak'?"

"Same thing except a little bit more personal."

Damn if she wasn't right again.

When his amusement waned, he said, "Cheer up, *sugar*. Look at it this way. You may have sent *my* life careening off into unexpected territory, but you're a lot better off."

There was no arguing that. She'd gone from being a penniless runaway cowering in a rain storm to being queen of a safe shelter with food and an escort who was also the sort of protector people want when they need protection.

Cann opened the door and found the light switch using the light of the phone. Nothing.

"No electricity either," Bud said drily.

"Stop your bellyaching. Women had children for thousands of years before Edison came on the scene."

"Yes. But they didn't have cell phones that need charging."

Cann had to admit that she had a point. He found a box of matches and lit the oil lamp that was sitting on the rustic table. It wasn't much light, but it was a small house. One room with a wood floor, bunk bed, table, two chairs, a rock fireplace, and a cowhide sofa that, oddly, would have sold for a lot of money in Beverly Hills.

Bud walked over to the kitchen sink and turned on the water. "Thank God for small favors," she said when it came on. "Guess that means the toilet will work. Speaking of that. Will you please make sure ther're no snakes in here so I can go to the bathroom?"

Cann was lighting a third candle. "Snakes, huh? They're more afraid of you than you are of them."

"Somehow I doubt that. And that's what people who are not afraid of snakes always say."

He chuckled. "Okay. Snake hunt."

"And I get the bottom bunk."

He looked at the bunk bed. "You think the top will hold my weight?"

"Well, there's a puzzle for you. Do I want to fall out of a second story bed or be crushed by an enormous biker dude?"

With a smile, Cann said, "Your choice," in an infuriatingly cavalier way.

Taking the oil lamp by the handle, Cann shone the light in every corner and cupboard before proclaiming, "All clear, your highness. The premises is viper free."

"Ok. If you're wrong, you'll have two deaths on your conscience."

"You don't know me well enough to think I have a conscience. You're assuming."

"Yes. I do. And no. I'm not," she said as she took a candle and closed the door. Toilet. Sink set in a prefab cabinet. Clawfoot tub which, again, would no doubt bring big bucks in Beverly Hills.

When she came out, Cann was making the last unloading trip. He'd put her bag on the lower bunk and the cooler in the kitchen end of the room.

She looked around. "It's kind of cold in here."

True to Brant's word, somebody had made sure the sheets were clean and there was a pile of firewood on the hearth.

Cann hesitated because chimney smoke is a long range visual signal that somebody's in residence and there would likely still be enough coals to make smoke when the sun came up. But, he supposed, Brant wouldn't have specifically mentioned having firewood stocked and left instructions encouraging him to make use of old school cooking and water heating if it wasn't safe.

"All right. I'll build you a fire. You hungry?"

She shook her head. "Just tired."

While Cann banked wood for a fire, Bud climbed up to the top bunk. She sat on her knees and wiggled around a little.

"What're you doin'?" Cann asked.

"Testing to make sure this bed will hold your ginormous ass up."

He laughed out loud. "First, I do not have a ginormous ass."

"Do," she said as she climbed down.

"Do not. Second, I was just kidding. Of course the bed will hold my perfectly formed manly body aloft."

It was her turn to laugh and she did it in the most scoffing way possible while secretly thinking that he did, in fact, have a perfectly formed manly body.

She slid under the covers.

"What're you doin' now?" he asked.

"Going to bed. Why are you so nosy about everything I do?"

"You're goin' to bed in your clothes?"

"It can't have escaped your attention that you met me on the run." Even though it was true that she had been a runaway, something about her use of the phrase 'on the run' struck him as hysterical. Probably because it conjured images of bad men in badlands. "What's so funny?"

"Nothing."

"I have a change of clothes and that's about it."

He nodded, feeling more serious. He'd been with Molly long enough to know that women are particular about hygiene and cleanliness and having the appropriate thing to wear for the appropriate event. He suspected that Bud usually wore pajamas or some version thereof and that doing without was part of her sacrifice. He had to admire the kid. She was committed to keeping that baby safe. She was probably gonna make somebody a good mama.

"Okay. Maybe it's just as well. Those quilts don't look all that warm."

He separated a bottled water from the plastic casing and set it down by her bed.

"Thank you," she said quietly, gripping the quilts so that they were pulled up over her chin. She was so unused to thoughtfulness directed at her, much less small kindnesses such as that and wasn't sure what to do with the feelings that came up in response.

"You're welcome," Cann said matter-of-factly as he turned away to set the screen in front of the fire.

DESPITE BEING IN her street clothes and in a strange place, Bud slept through the night. That was an event that had been a lot less common since she'd been pregnant. She woke to the sounds of Cann rekindling the fire then scrambled up and hurried toward the toilet before it was too late.

The relief she felt from emptying her bladder was almost a pleasure in itself.

She looked in the mirror and wished she'd thought to bring her bag in with her. She cracked the door open.

"Johns?"

"Yeah?"

"Would you hand me my bag?"

He glanced toward the bed where she'd stowed her bag under the bottom bunk. "No good mornin'?"

After a slight hesitation, she sniffed and said, "Sure. Good mornin'," trying to remember if she'd ever before in her life, even once, been expected to utter a courtesy considered so common by so many.

After pulling the bag through the crack in the door, she brushed teeth, washed face and tamed the wild hair. By the time she was finished with that she was, to her amazement, smelling bacon cooking.

When she drew near, she saw that Cann had set an iron skillet off to the side of the fire after forming a section with just the amount of heat he needed.

"Want coffee?" he said.

Her eyes traveled the hearth until they found the pot. It looked like it might have been red at one time, but had been blackened and encrusted with the flame and soot of many such mornings without modern convenience. She briefly wondered who the other people were and why they had sought refuge in the small rock house on the Mexican border.

"Yes," she said in a voice that sounded too rough to be hers. She cleared her throat. "Is there something I can do to help?"

"Yep," he said without looking up. "Go get us one of those rolls of biscuits out of the cooler." As he was using a fork to turn the bacon over, the grease made a loud popping noise. Cann hissed and brought the heel of his hand up to his mouth. "Christ. That hurts."

Bud hurried to the cooler and grabbed a handful of ice. When she returned she slapped it on Cann's burn.

"Here. You hold this. I'll take care of the bacon."

Cann looked at her like he was seeing her for the first time. Sometimes she didn't seem like a kid at all. Dutifully, he took the ice in his big hand and held it on the burn.

"This is pretty clever," she said. "Cooking food in a fireplace."

"Yeah. Imagine that. Quest for fire."

"Well it may not be new to humanity, but it's new to me."

By the time Cann walked over to the cooler, the ice had melted. He took one of the cans of biscuits out, greased the second skillet and placed them in the pan snuggled up close together, unlike what the directions said to do. But of course, the directions talked about baking in ovens.

He brought the pan of biscuits back to the fire and set it off to the side where, he estimated, it would be exposed to just the right amount of heat.

"Bacon's done," she said as she forked it onto the wood tray that had been lined with a paper sack and paper towels.

"Okay." He used the ancient oven mitt to pick up the

skillet, walked it outside a ways from the house and dumped the excess grease into a rocky crevice, leaving just the tiniest bit in the pan.

When he returned she said, "What's next?"

He nodded toward the kitchen area. "There's a bowl over there with some eggs whisked and ready to go. Bring it over here if you please."

When she saw that he intended to dump the beaten eggs into the skillet, she said, "NOOOOOO!" He looked up at her and smiled just before pouring the eggs into the bacon grease. "How could you do that?"

"You'll see."

"I'll see what? Inedible eggs."

He laughed. "You know you have the makings of a drama queen."

"Do not."

"Do."

"Oh my God! Look what you've done to those perfectly good perfectly yellow eggs. They're disgusting!"

"They're not disgusting. They're called dirty eggs."

"And that's exactly what they look like! No thanks."

"Tastin' before judgin'."

"Is that a policy statement?"

"I don't know what a policy statement is."

"It's a rule you live by."

"I don't make rules about food, but if I did, that would be one of 'em. Up. Biscuits are ready."

"Are those plates and forks clean?"

"Caretaker. Everything's fine. Just take the bacon over

there and sit down at the, uh, table."

"Do we have any juice in that ice chest?"

"I think I saw some. You're welcome to hunt around."

While Cann carried a skillet of eggs and a skillet of biscuits, Bud was bending over the ice chest looking for juice. One look at her heart-shaped derriere pointed in that position had his cock twitching in his pants. He scolded himself for the inappropriateness of that and looked away, suddenly on a mission to find the salt and pepper.

"Eureka!" she shouted, holding up a pint bottle of orange juice like it was a prize. "Want some?"

He could see by the look on her face that she was hoping he'd say no. He shook his head after biting into a piece of thick slab bacon and used a booted foot to invite her to sit by pushing her chair out and away from the table.

As she dropped into the chair he spooned a large helping of 'dirty' eggs onto her plate.

"Hey!" she said. "You said taste. Not consume a dozen eggs."

"There's not more than two eggs there, missy. And you need the protein."

She gaped. "Now it's missy?"

He chuckled. "This mornin' it is. Keep up."

"I'll see what I can do, pumpkin."

He laughed out loud. She'd done it again. Made him forget for a second that he was a hapless man overdue for a meeting with suicide.

Bud took a long, long look at a tiny bit of scrambled eggs on her fork before she put it in her mouth, but her expression quickly changed from revulsion for the food to respect for Cann.

"This is good." She said it like it was a miracle.

"Yeah. I know."

While Bud looked on, Cann used a spatula to separate a biscuit and delivered it to her plate. She supposed the last time she'd been fed by another person was before her earliest memory. He rose and grabbed the open butter container he'd used to grease the biscuit pan.

"Hunted around in there." He meant the ice chest. "But I didn't see any jam or jelly or honey."

"Butter's fine."

"Okay."

She took a bite of hot buttered biscuit and moaned softly. "This is so good. I don't know. Maybe the best food I ever had."

"Well, you know what they say."

"What?"

"That the best food is the food you don't have to cook yourself." He chuckled.

"Yeah." She grinned. "Might be something to that."

Bud didn't hear anything, but Cann's head suddenly jerked toward the front of the house. It only took his long legs three strides to reach the windows. He relaxed visibly.

"Must be Maria."

"How do you know?"

"Because the vehicle is not exactly this year's model. Or last year's."

Bud nodded. "I get it."

By the time Maria was knocking at the door, they were finished with breakfast and clearing the table.

After hellos, Cann had a conversation with Maria in Spanish. She appeared to be in her forties and had an engaging smile which she turned toward Bud three times during the conversation with Cannon Johns.

"What size shoes do you wear?"

"Seven. Why?"

"Maria's goin' to go into Presidio and get you a pair of hikin' boots, just in case we end up walkin' around. You can't wear those…" He waved at her feet. "Whatever those are."

"Keds."

"Like I said… whatever. Is there anything else you need from town? More juice?"

"Snickers."

He looked at Maria, who nodded. Bud assumed that meant Snickers is Snickers in any language.

"And shampoo! Something that smells nice."

After another brief exchange Cann handed Maria a couple of large bills. She nodded at Bud and smiled on her way out the door.

"So. You speak Spanish."

"Well, yes, sugar. I'm from Texas."

"*I'm* from Texas and I don't speak Spanish."

"I don't know how that's even possible? Didn't you say you're from El Paso?"

"Yeah."

"Then you'd have to be workin' at not learnin' it."

"Not true."

"You don't know any Spanish?"

"Gracias. Mucho. Grande. Si. No. Señorita."

He stared for several seconds. "That's just sad. How do you expect to get a job here without speaking *any* Spanish?"

"There are always other people around who do?"

"That's ridiculous." She laughed. "What's funny?"

"I don't know. The way you say 'ridiculous'. It just seems so out of place on your bad ass bikeryness."

"I don't need to tell you that's not a word. Right?"

"Okay. Since there is nothing else to do here, why don't you teach me Spanish?"

He seemed to be considering that.

"I might. What do you have to offer in exchange?" Her smile fell and he realized how she'd taken that. "No. Not that. Something to teach me that I don't already know."

"Oh. Okay." She looked around the room. "Wow. Seems like you already know how to cook."

"Got it covered."

"I know how to shoot."

Though he seemed interested, he didn't ask. "Got that covered, too."

She looked over at her bag. She didn't have a lot of

stuff with her, but she did have a deck of bicycle cards. "You know how to play cards?"

"Of course."

"Gin rummy?"

"No. Poker."

"Okay then. I'll teach you gin rummy." When he said nothing, she offered, "Or the chicken dance."

"I don't know what the chicken dance is, but I'm pretty sure I'm not interested in learning it."

"Tastin' before judgin'," she said, throwing his words back at him.

They had nothing else to do to pass the time so playing cards was as good as anything.

"Gin rummy it is. Payment for Spanish lessons."

By mid-afternoon Bud was working on ten common conversational phrases. Cann laughed at her accent, but all in all, he wasn't a bad teacher.

They ate junk food and enjoyed long periods of companionable silence playing gin rummy.

"It's not fair that you're better than I am at the game I taught *you*!" Bud complained.

Cann laughed at her. "It's just luck. Come on. Next time you'll get better cards." She didn't get better cards, but continued to be vocal about not liking it. "You're competitive," he said, like it was a revelation. "Also a sore loser."

"Am not."

"Are."

Maria returned before dinner with bags full of goodies that included a cell phone adaptor for the truck and a couple of changes of clothes for Bud. Tee shirts, jeans, socks, underwear, pajamas. Hiking boots with thick tire tread soles and leather up to the ankles.

"Get your dirty laundry together," Cann said. "Maria's going to wash our stuff and bring it back tomorrow."

"Really?" Bud looked from Cann to Maria and back like she was sure he was lying. The idea of someone else washing her clothes was so alien to her that she was having a hard time picturing it.

Cann looked at her like she was slow. "Yeah. Really." When she didn't move, he said, "You need help?"

She shook her head. "No. Just a sec." She grabbed a plastic bag from the kitchen and shoved everything that she wasn't wearing into the stash. When she handed it to Maria, she said, "Thank you."

"You can do better than that," Cann said.

It took Bud a couple of seconds to understand what he meant. She grinned at Maria. "I mean gracias."

Maria grinned and nodded her head. "De nada."

BUD TOOK THE top off the shampoo and inhaled. Green apples. "Damn it."

"What's the problem?" Cann asked.

"Now I have this great-smelling shampoo and no hot water."

"I can get you enough hot water so that, when you add cold, you'll have about eight inches of warm water in that tub in there."

She blinked at Cann a couple of times before saying, "I'll take it." He nodded and set to work pulling out the two big soup pots in the cabinet. "And thank you," she said a little more softly.

"You're welcome. You get your bath stuff together. It'll take a little bit."

He put more wood on the fire and filled the pots.

"You're kind of handy. You know that?"

Cann wasn't sure if that was a compliment or gratitude, but it sounded like it might be a bit of both. "Can be," he answered with a small measure of masculine pride.

EVEN THOUGH THE bath was far from ideal, Bud emerged feeling clean and renewed, with towel dried hair and skin that felt pristine. Cann took one look at her and burst out laughing.

"Don't blame me," Bud said. "*I'm* not the one who speaks Spanish. All I've got to say is that now I understand why Maria kept smiling at me."

Bud stood there in Spongebob Squarepants pajamas with a hand on one hip and a challenging posture. On the one hand, the print was beyond silly. On the other, the lightweight knit outlined every inch of Bud's lithe young figure and brought attention to the fact that her stomach was still ironing-board flat.

"What are you looking at?" she said.

His eyes came back up to hers quickly. "Just noticin'

that you aren't, um, showing."

"If I was far enough along to be showing, then it would be too late to…"

"Yeah." He nodded. "So how far along are you?"

"Eight weeks. I think."

"How did he find out?"

"I told him. I thought it would be better to tell him why I wasn't starting school this semester than to pay the money and drop out."

Cann regarded her thoughtfully. "Most kids your age wouldn't think like that."

"Will you stop calling me a kid?" Normally she would have left it at that, but the part of her that recognized that at the very least she owed the big handsome biker courtesy for being her unlikely rescuer urged her to add, "Please."

"You know someday you're gonna wish folks thought of you as younger."

Without pause she said, "Then I'll ask them to call me a kid."

He chuckled, shaking his head. "It's hard to think of you as a grown woman when you're wearin' those pajamas." It was a lie. Anatomically she was all woman, but it sounded plausible.

She looked down at the pajamas. "Clothes don't make the, um, person."

After taking a sip of coffee, he said, "Cannot argue that." He pulled the phone out of his pocket and looked at the face. "I'm going to go run the truck long enough to charge the phone. Shouldn't take too long. You be okay here?"

Bud cocked her head at the question. After a lifetime of taking care of herself, it was odd to have someone ask if she'd be okay. She tried to remember if her father had ever asked that short and simple question and couldn't say that he had.

When Cann looked closely at her young flawless face, waiting patiently for an answer, he saw for the first time that the eyes looking back belonged to someone who was older than the edge of eighteen. On the inside.

"Of course," she said, with the maturity of a woman. Not a girl.

And he wondered how he'd failed to read the situation correctly. He was a hundred years old walking around in a twenty-six-year-old body. She was twenty-six walking around in an eighteen-year-old body.

As he rose to his feet, he ducked his head in acknowledgement then set the coffee cup down on the table, and walked to the shed that was temporarily housing the truck.

Bud noticed the instantly empty feeling of the house when she was left alone. She had known that Cann was a big guy surrounded by a big invisible presence, but experiencing the difference in atmospheric environment after that presence withdrew was breathtaking.

That's what they mean when people talk about someone being a force of nature, she thought.

She crawled under the quilts and stared at the fire.

Even though Cann wasn't in the house, knowing he was close by gave her a sense of peace and security like she'd never known. As drowsiness began to claim her, she admonished herself not to get attached. Cannon Johns was a man unlike any she'd ever known or known of. But her time with him was temporary. Six days. And she couldn't get attached.

Something woke her hours later. Still facing the fire, she opened her eyes a slit and watched Cann as he zipped up a black backpack before setting it by the front door. She watched as he undressed, draping his clothes over the cowhide sofa until he was wearing nothing but dark boxers. He was magnificently larger than life clothed or unclothed. He was no Abercrombie model. There was not the slightest hint of softness anywhere on the planes of his body or in his expression. He was hard. Rugged.

When he turned toward the bunk bed, she shut her eyes. When the bunk moved as he pulled himself up, she smiled. She didn't know why. There was no reason for it.

BUD'S FIRST THOUGHT, before she even opened her eyes, was that bacon was cooking and that it might possibly be one of the world's best aromas. She turned over to see what was going on.

Cann was crouched in front of the hearth tending to breakfast.

She got to her feet quietly and ran to the bathroom before he could see that, when she first woke up, she looked more like a zombie than a young woman coming into her prime. As she slammed the door behind her, she heard him say, "Mornin'."

She'd stowed her bag in the bath because it made more sense to keep everything there. After brushing her teeth, she tamed the hair that had still been damp when she'd gone to bed, by wetting it and pulling it into French braids. She hadn't worn makeup for the past two days. She told herself she was going for the wholesome outdoorsy look.

The jeans Maria bought her were slightly baggy, but the chance of having them fit perfectly without trying on was essentially nil. All things considered, too big was better than too small. She pulled the long-sleeved knit Henley over her head. It was a lavender blue that made her eyes pop. Not that she was interested in such things.

The hiking boots weren't something she would have bought for herself, but they were surprisingly comfortable and made her feel confident and powerful in a completely inexplicable way.

When she opened the door, Cann looked her direction. His eyes scanned her quickly up and down.

"Bacon and eggs?" she asked.

"Nope," he said without giving up any more information.

"Cat got your tongue?"

He smirked at her. "BLTs."

"Sandwiches for breakfast?"

"That a problem?"

"No. It's actually kind of cool. I like BLTs."

"Maria brought lettuce and tomato. Oranges grown here in the valley. They're good. Sweet. Not like the ones that ripen in trucks and trains on the way to grocery stores."

"Got mayo?"

"How do you make a BLT without mayo?"

She smiled. "I don't know. Just making conversation." She watched as he turned bacon over. "So what do you want to do today?"

He snorted as he walked by her headed for the kitchen with a plate of fresh cooked bacon. After setting it down on the small kitchen counter, he began assembling slices of tomato and large Boston lettuce leaves. Bud became captivated by his hands. Aside from the sheer size of them, which was impressive in itself, they had the look of capability. They were tanned and weathered from years of riding a motorcycle, probably without sunscreen.

She found herself wondering what those hands would feel like caressing her bare skin.

"What I want to do today… Well, I'd like to start with a few laps in the heated pool. Maybe have some Bloody Marys brought to me while I'm drying off in my thick white robe. After that, maybe a spin through the mountains in the Lamborghini."

She took a seat at the table shaking her head. "Not gonna happen. It's not running and there's not a qualified repair within five hundred miles. The Bentley is running though. And I feel like electric blue today."

"Bentley it is," Cann said. "Maybe we'll stop at that

little roadside spot that specializes in fried calamari."

"And margaritas. Don't forget the important part."

"Sorry, sugar. Even if you were old enough to drink, doctor says nuh-uh."

"All right. Forget the margaritas."

"Hell, no. I'm still havin' margaritas." He chuckled as he set two large cut-in-half sandwiches down on the table and smothered them in potato chips.

"That's mean," she said.

"Orrrrrrr…"

"Or what?" She couldn't wait a second longer to take a bite. Those sandwiches looked like her idea of an ultimate fantasy meal.

"Or we could clean up. Go do some target shooting. Play some cards and work on your Spanish."

Chewing while pretending to look thoughtful, Bud said, "Yeah. That sounds good, too."

THEY WALKED ABOUT thirty yards away from the house and set up a makeshift target in front of a hill so that they'd basically be shooting into dirt and rock. Bud wasn't kidding about being good with a gun.

When she hit her target six times in a row, she threw Cann a smug look. He smiled and nodded, which she took as high praise. Standing so close to him, she noticed the two days of red beard scruff coming in.

"Your beard looks like it's on fire in direct sunlight." He immediately reached up and scrubbed his hand across his jaw. "It's kind of pretty."

He barked out a laugh. "Well, that's a new one." He shook his head and repeated, "Pretty," like that was the most outlandish thing he'd ever heard. He was obligated, according to the code of men's men, to protest the word 'pretty'. So he did. But he also seemed to enjoy the compliment.

On the walk back to the house, Cann said, "So it looks like your old man taught you *somethin'*."

"You mean shooting?" She shrugged. "When he was around, he taught me stuff he knew."

"You love him?"

"Mixed feelings. He's my daddy, but tryin' to take this baby from me just isn't right. He's not God. Shouldn't be his decision. I mean, don't get me wrong, I'm not one of those people who wants to tell everybody else what they should be doing with their business." She looked at Cann for his reaction, but he gave none. "Thank you for…"

When she didn't finish the sentence, he said, "For what?"

"For taking care of my baby when you could be having a Bloody Mary by the heated pool in your thick white robe." Cann laughed out loud and the sound of it was good. So good it made her nipples hard. Trying to ignore that, she said, "Do you even own a white robe?"

He shook his head, "No, darlin'. I do not own a white robe. Never have. Never will."

After a few steps, she said, "So we're back to darlin'." He chuckled. "Could you, um, really get into trouble for this? Helping me, I mean?"

"We've been over this. Your daddy's a Ranger. So what do you think?"

That was a fine example of a rhetorical question. It was a question that imprinted on her heart. Cannon Johns had made a sacrifice to care for her. At the least it had cost him a week. At the most it could cost him his freedom.

It was an uncommon deed, the sort of thing that could never be repaid and she had no idea why he was putting himself in such a precarious position for a strange girl. With no promise of personal benefit or gain.

As they stepped onto the porch, she said, "Why are you doing this?"

He closed the screen door that he'd opened a few inches, looked down at his boots, and sighed. "I couldn't save my own…" his breath hitched, "little girl. But I think I can save yours."

Bud waited until his gaze came up. She tried to push all the gratitude she felt into her eyes so that he would understand that she recognized what he was doing, the chance he was taking.

Then she smiled and said, "What makes you think it's a girl?"

He smiled in return. "Don't you?"

THEY HAD ORANGES and Snickers for lunch. Afterward Cann went out to the shed, turned on the truck, plugged in the phone, and called Brant.

"Yeah?" Brant answered on the first ring.

"Checking in."

"They were here the night you left. Haven't heard anything else, but the story's still runnin' on TV. People are kind of caught up in speculation about you and the kid."

"She's not a kid." Cann almost couldn't believe he'd said that. It had come out fast, without thinking, and he wasn't even sure he believed it.

There was a pause on the other end. "I told you not to touch her," Brant started.

"I'm not!"

"Okay. Just keep your head down for, what is it? Three more days."

"Yeah. Three days."

"Call me when you're headed back."

"All right."

CANN GAVE BUD Spanish lessons while mercilessly beating her at gin rummy, but made it up to her by proclaiming they were having chili dogs for supper. They used wire coat hangers to roast the weenies then stuffed them into buns with turkey chili, mustard, and cheddar cheese.

She made yummy sounds so comical that she had Cann smiling through dinner. Afterward, he said, "My turn for the bath tonight."

She smiled. "Okay. What can I do to help?"

"What did you have in mind?" he asked playfully in a way that could have been interpreted as flirtatious.

On impulse, she decided to test the waters, so to

speak. "You heat and carry the water. I'll undress you." She wiggled her eyebrows.

He couldn't help but laugh. The idea of being pursued and propositioned by an underage pregnant girl under his protection was too outrageous to be anything but funny.

"What's so funny?"

"You."

"Me? I'm not being funny, Johns. Are you gay?"

"Am I gay?" His eyebrows went up and his forehead wrinkled.

"Yes. That was the question. I once heard that, when people repeat a question they're doing it to give them time to think up a lie. Are you trying to think up a lie, Johns?"

He couldn't believe he was letting this child put him on the defensive. "Look. It's not that you're not attractive. You are. Of course you are. It's that you're pregnant, seventeen, and in a position to feel like you owe me. When you add all that together, it's a bad combination for entanglements. And that is all we're going to say about it. Except that, I know you were joking. Right?"

She decided retreat was the best course of action. "Right. Joking. Joking. Totally joking. Just kidding around. Ha. Ha."

"That's what I thought."

That night Cann dreamed that Molly and the baby were in a field of bluebonnets on a bright spring day with an impossibly blue sky and an impossibly yellow sun. Molly blew him a kiss. She was talking, saying something, but he couldn't make out what. When she picked up the baby and turned away, Cann felt panicked, even in his dream.

He tried to run after her, but couldn't move. She turned around and began talking again. He still didn't hear what she was saying, but he was left with the distinct impression that it was, "We love you. Now let go of us and live your life. We're moving on to the next adventure. You should, too."

When she walked away, she disappeared and there was nothing left in the dream but the bluebonnets lit by an impossibly yellow sun hanging in an impossibly blue sky.

Cann woke up feeling different. He couldn't say how. He didn't know how. He just knew things had changed somehow.

CHAPTER SEVEN

It was mid-morning when Cann thought he heard the sound of a different engine. Not Maria's car.

He rushed to the window and looked out. "Somebody's coming. Let's go."

He reached down and grabbed the backpack he'd so carefully stowed by the front door and ran for the shed without waiting to see if she was following. He knew he could pick her up on the way out if needs be.

She was right behind him and jumped into the passenger seat as he was starting the truck. He knew he didn't have time to back out.

"Got your seatbelt on?" he said.

"Yes."

"Put your head down."

She did so instantly, and just before he drove right through the back of the shed. He circled in front of the house and headed cross country for the river. They were about fifty yards ahead of the two Ranger SUVs. Cann didn't stop at the river's edge but drove right in. They got about one third of the way across when the truck bogged down in mud.

"Come on," he said. He jumped out, but she wasn't strong enough to get the passenger door open against the current of the waist-high water. He pulled the backpack on, jerked her door open and helped her out.

The Rangers were standing on the bank of the river. One of them fired a gun. Cann suspected it had been fired into the air, but couldn't be sure. One of them had a bullhorn.

"Bring the girl back or we'll shoot," he said.

Cann didn't think they'd shoot at a Ranger's daughter, but the sons-of-bitches might be that crazy. So he picked her up and cradled her in his arms. If they were going to shoot, they'd hit him. And not her.

Oddly, those were the random thoughts going through his mind as he was wading across the Rio Grande ready to give his life for a girl who'd been a stranger a few days before. Big eyes hiding behind a Mountain Dew machine.

Christ. Life is strange.

He had to hand it to the little mother-to-be in his arms. She hadn't made a sound. Not a whimper. She'd done what she was told fearlessly.

He didn't hear any more gunshots. And he didn't hear any more instructions. He suspected they'd figured out that they might as well save their breath. Nobody was getting their hands on Bud until she was eighteen goddamn years old.

After they walked out of the river, they turned around and looked at the Rangers on the other side. They were watching, but it was clear that, as Brant had said, they weren't going to do anything else.

When he set Bud on her feet, out of curiosity he put two fingers on her neck. Her heart was pumping like they were being chased by Godzilla. Yes. She was naturally born battle worthy and going to be a great mama to some lucky kid.

Cann pulled out his phone and got their location. Then, turning his back on the river, he made a burner phone call.

"Yeah?" Brant answered.

The relief Cann felt hearing that the phone had picked up service was indescribable. He closed his eyes for a second.

"Just like you said, Prez. They won't follow across the river."

"Jesus."

"Yeah. Mary and Joseph, too. Arnold's truck is a little less than halfway across. Maybe Maria knows somebody who can get it out tonight and give it a new incarnation."

"You're gonna owe Arnold a ton of money."

"Well, what's it good for anyway? We're three miles northeast of Ojinaga."

"Hang on. Heading due south will run you into Highway 16. I'll have somebody out there looking for you. If you don't make connections before you get to Ojinaga, go to the Alsuper on Avenue Trasvina y Retes. They'll pick you up there."

"Okay."

"Be careful. If you get to the Alsuper before my contact finds you, let her have bottled water and the fruit after you wash it. Nothing else unless it's packaged in the U.S."

"Yep. Got it." He looked at Bud. "We're hoofin' it."

"Okay." She smiled as if he'd just said she'd won free pizza for a year.

"Brant's sendin' somebody out to look for us, but we've got to get to the highway and it's a ways. If they don't find us on the road, we'll make contact in town."

She nodded. "Why'd you carry me?"

He looked down at his feet. Those boots would never be the same and he doubted the walk was going to be fun. "Heard a shot. I knew it was unlikely they'd shoot at us. But every now and then a crazy sneaks into law enforcement or somebody makes a mistake."

"Yeah, but why'd you carry me?"

He looked up into those amazing violet eyes and got transfixed for a minute. "Come on. We don't have time to stand here jabberin'."

"Jabberin'?"

"You heard me."

"I wasn't jabberin'. And that's kind of insulting. You know that?"

It took them almost three hours to get to Federal 16. It would have been a forty-five minute walk on pavement, but cross country is something entirely different.

After they'd been walking for about an hour Bud said, "Remind me to thank you properly for these boots. I'd be in a world of shit makin' this walk in those Keds." She paused. "They were cute though."

She pretty much kept up the small talk and prattle for the duration. It might have bothered some guys, but Cann found it strangely comforting. He also admired the fact that she was doggedly cheerful in the face of events that would cause open complaining from most women.

"There aren't any rattlesnakes out here, right?" Cann just laughed. "But you've got that pistol loaded, right?"

"Right."

He didn't want to mention that there were a lot of things more dangerous than rattlesnakes that close to the border.

When they finally stepped onto the paved road, Bud said, "Yay. We made it. Which way?"

Cann just pointed east and started walking. He had to constantly remind himself to slow his pace because his legs were so much longer than hers.

There were no cars. Just miles of blacktop, scrub brush, sand, and hills. The ground wouldn't grow crops or even enough edible flora to feed goats. It was a part of the country that many Texans called God-forsaken.

Fifteen minutes after they'd been on the road, a red pickup approached going west. Cann eased the backpack off, unzipped it and slid his hand inside until the pistol filled his palm and his finger was on the safety. The truck slowed and two guys took a long look at them, but didn't stop. No doubt two gringos walking on 16 was a sight to see. The guys in the truck would be telling that story for years and people would laugh and say they'd had too much tequila, that such a thing simply would not, could not, did not happen.

The second vehicle that slowed was their guy.

Through the open window of an ancient Toyota that had badly needed paint years before, the driver said, "Sanchuery Jahns."

Cann nodded. To Bud, he said, "I'm gettin' in the front passenger seat. You get in back but not until after I'm in the car."

She nodded.

Once they were both in the car, the driver made a call and handed the phone to Cann.

"Yeah?" Cann said.

It was Brant. "There's a hotel in Ojinaga. Stay there tonight. Tomorrow morning somebody'll come get you and drive you to Del Rio. We have friends there. They'll take care of you till birthday Friday. I'll let you know what to do when you get there."

"All right. And, Prez…"

"Yeah?"

"Thank you."

"No need to thank me, fuckup. I'm gonna take this outta your hide in good time."

The Ojinaga Hotel wasn't half bad for thirty seven dollars a night. The clerk gave them both looks related to having jeans that were wet from the waist down in Bud's case, thigh down in Cann's. Cann got a room for the two of them with two double beds. It had weird murals of a cityscape on one wall and the silhouette of a long haired dancing woman on another, but it appeared to be reasonably clean.

"Hey. This is a lot better than the place where you picked me up," Bud said.

"I did not pick you up."

"Well, what would you call it?"

"I did pick you up, but when you say it like that…" He looked away. "Never mind."

"I can't wait to take a real shower. Even if I don't have any clean clothes to put on. You think our boots will dry out by tomorrow?"

"Doubt it."

"I don't want you to freak out, but I need to hang these wet clothes up. So I'm going to put a towel on."

"Why would I freak out?"

"Because you've made it so clear you're not interested in me."

"I'm not going to freak out at the sight of you in a towel, sugar. But I've got a better idea."

"What?"

"There's a supermercado a couple of blocks away. If you're up for a walk, we can go get some dry clothes and some stuff to eat."

"Let's go." She was already waiting at the door when she finished that sentence.

TWO HOURS LATER they were back in the room with clothes that were cheap but dry, bottles of water, fresh fruit, specialty crackers and peanut butter from across the border.

Bud took a shower before dining on oranges and peanut butter crackers while Cann marveled at how adaptable and upbeat she was. Considering all the changes she'd gone through in a scant three days, it was amazing how she took it all in stride.

"What are you thinking about?" she said.

He refocused his attention on her. "That you're not like most girls. You've handled yourself really well." He paused and looked over at her. "Admirably."

"Wow, Johns. That sounds a lot like a compliment."

"Intended."

"Then thank you."

"Welcome."

"You think there're any English shows on TV?"

Cann smirked. "Go ahead and look. But your Spanish is never gonna get better that way."

She did find reruns of "I Love Lucy" with Spanish subtitles. She curled up under the covers and was asleep in minutes. Cann put down the book he'd brought along in the backpack and looked at her. She seemed younger when she was asleep, all the cares and strain gone from her face with nothing left behind but the flawlessness of youth. He turned off the TV and got under the covers of his own bed.

"I'm not leaving any of this stuff behind. What if we don't have a chance to get more?"

She was talking about three bottles of water, two oranges, a half-eaten jar of peanut butter and a few crackers.

"Suit yourself, but if you're bringin' it, you're carryin' it."

"Fine by me, but then you don't get any."

Cann rolled his eyes.

A guy named Marco had shown up five minutes before and identified himself as their driver. They followed Marco down the hall without being self-conscious about ill-fitting clothes. They had other problems. Like the brand new dry socks that had gone damp within minutes of pulling on boots. Their boots wouldn't be completely dry for days and, even then, would never be comfortable again.

BUD KNEW THE drill. Cann got into the front seat then Bud claimed the back. When they were loaded into the nondescript sedan, they turned west. Cann said, "Del Rio's the other way, friend."

Marco said, "Going to Chihuahua, señor."

"Chihuahua? Why?"

"Closest airfield."

The Chihuahua airport was just an hour's drive. It was small, but new. They didn't stop but went past to a row of private small craft hangars. A four passenger prop plane was waiting on the tarmac looking surprisingly spiffy with bright yellow paint and spotless windshield.

When Bud got out of the car, she hesitated.

"What's wrong?" Cann asked.

She stepped close to Cann so she could speak without being overheard. "I've never flown before."

Cann looked from her to the plane and back again. He smiled. "Then it's gonna be a helluva first experience. Flyin' in big commercial jets isn't really flyin'. This is. You're gonna love it."

She figured she hadn't gone wrong by trusting the big biker so far. So she might as well be all in and see it through. No matter what. So she pushed the fluttering in her stomach down and told her feet to walk forward.

The pilot spoke to Cann in Spanish.

Cann said, "You need to go to the ladies'? Cause it's gonna be about four and a half hours in the air."

Her eyes flicked to the pilot and back to Cann. "Yeah. Please."

When she emerged from the bare bones hangar unisex toilet, she climbed in behind the pilot. She'd been told to sit there to equalize the weight. Cann would sit in front with the pilot. She supposed that meant that she and the pilot together weighed about the same as Cann. Although the backpack and groceries were stowed on the empty seat next to her.

The next few hours of flying low across northern Mexico was something she would never forget for the rest of her life. And Cannon Johns was exactly right. The trip from the city of Chihuahua to Del Rio was *really* flying.

After a couple of hours the pilot announced that they had just flown over the state line and were in Coahuila.

An hour after that they flew over the Maderas del Carmen range and the winds buffeted the plane about. Bud didn't feel frightened by it. When the plane dropped a few feet leaving her stomach aloft, she laughed out loud.

They landed, taxied, and pulled to a stop just steps away from a newish silver van. A young twenty-something guy stood by the sliding door wearing a smile and a leather vest with patches. He'd clearly left the door open for Bud and Cann.

Another man wearing a cut approached and offered his hand to Cann.

"I'm Gerson. Driving you this fine day."

"Thank you." Cann shook the man's hand then turned to Bud. "You good?"

She shook her head. "Restroom," she said under her breath.

"Lady needs a pit stop."

Gerson turned and told the guy leaning against the van to show the woman to the toilet. Cann nodded at Bud to indicate it would be okay for her to go without him.

Cann and Gerson chatted about the weather until Bud rejoined them.

As Bud climbed into the backseat Cann nodded to the guy who was apparently riding 'shotgun' before joining her. The van was luxurious, custom outfitted. Cann wondered if it was bulletproofed, but it would have been insulting to ask. So he didn't.

When the van reached the road that would take them into the city, they were joined by about thirty-five bikers wearing cuts like Gerson's. The rockers said Demonios de Viento. *Wind demons.*

Half of the bikers went in front of the van. The other half pulled in behind in a formation that had apparently been worked out ahead of time.

Bud said nothing, but raised her eyebrows as if silently asking about the exchange. Cann shrugged in response then impulsively reached over, put his hand on hers and gave a little reassuring squeeze.

When Bud looked from Cann's face down to the big hand resting on top of hers, he quickly pulled back and looked out the window.

"What's all this?" Cann asked.

"Full honors," Gerson replied. "You and the lovely lady must be a very big deal."

Cann laughed softly. "No. That would be my Prez, I guess."

"These days Del Rio can be unpredictable. We've been told to make sure you arrive safely. And that is what we will do."

"Where're we goin'?"

Gerson looked surprised. "You don't know?"

"I'm a soldier. I was told that people would get us to Del Rio. I wasn't briefed on logistics."

"I see. Well, seems the two of you will be privileged to be guests of one of Del Rio's most important families."

Twenty minutes later they pulled up to a walled estate with armed guards posted at the gates. The van was allowed inside. The bikers stayed where they were.

After a couple of minutes of winding driveway, they pulled up in front of a parking court with a fountain in the middle. The hacienda-style house with cream stucco walls and red tile roof was palatial.

A man opened half of an impressive double door entry and a woman swept through. She descended the steps with the intention of greeting guests it seemed.

Bud was instantly on feminine alert. The woman was impeccably styled from the top of her slicked back hair to the red bottoms of her two thousand dollar Jimmy Choo high heeled sandals. She wore red lipstick to match her red suit with gold buttoned lapels that swept into a deep vee neck just a little too revealing for Bud's taste. The suit was custom tailored so that it hugged curves and waist like a second skin.

When the woman ignored her and began fawning over Cann, Bud disliked her even more. She wasn't paying attention to what was being said until Cann turned to her. "Bud. This is Señora Gutierrez."

The woman made a point of looking surprised, like she hadn't noticed Bud had been standing there the whole time. Bud offered her hand to Señora Gutierrez politely. The señora responded by pinching two of Bud's fingers between two of her own for a pointedly brief two seconds. Bud was tempted to laugh at the bizarre behavior, but remained quiet and watchful.

The woman was talking to Cann, who said, "My companion is just learning Spanish. Perhaps we could speak English so that she will understand?"

The woman looked at Bud and did another scan from top to bottom and back again while making a point of conveying disdain. "Of course." She then proceeded to speak to Bud with aggravating precision and slow pace. "Welcome to our home. Please come inside."

Bud's eyes flew to Cann as she asked the silent question, *"Is she for real?"*

Cann's eyes were alight with amusement. He pressed his lips together and shook his head ever so slightly. As they climbed the steps, she turned and said, "That will be all, Gerson."

Gerson's eyes widened slightly like he couldn't imagine that she had the nerve to dismiss him like a servant. He exchanged a brief look with Cann and turned to go.

Bud had never been in a restaurant or hotel with twenty-foot ceilings, much less a house. Looking through the windows, Bud could see that the house was built in a rectangle around a central courtyard that featured manicured gardens and a fountain.

The furnishings and appointments were lavish enough to be bordering on the obscene, everything in variations of white, cream, brown, and rust.

"This way," Señora Gutierrez motioned to the grand staircase and began to ascend swaying her hips back and forth in an exaggerated way.

As they began to climb side by side, Bud touched Cann's arm. When he looked over, she mocked Señora Gutierrez's hip movement. Before he could stop himself

Cann barked out a laugh.

The señora stopped and turned to look at them.

Cann said, "Sorry, Señora. Bud was just making fun of my boots."

Satisfied that a joke was not being had at her expense, the lady of the house led them to the second floor. They turned right and walked until they reached the end of the hallway.

"I hope this is to your liking, Señor Johns," she said.

"Call me Cann. This is wonderful. Thank you."

She lowered her eyelashes in response then turned to Bud. "Your room is this way." She gestured toward the other end of the hall.

"Hold on," Cann said. "She stays with me."

"Oh?" The señora looked surprised. "Forgive me. I was led to believe that she is a child."

"Until the day after tomorrow," he replied. "In any case, she's under my protection. I'm her guardian and she'll sleep where I can see her. Even if we have to sleep outside."

There was no mistaking that he was serious.

Bud had remained still and quiet through the exchange. Though she didn't show it outwardly, she was grateful that she wasn't going to be separated from Cann.

"Of course that won't be necessary," Gutierrez said. "We have another room with two beds. Will that suit your needs?"

"Perfectly," Cann said simply. "Thank you."

Gutierrez pressed her lips together in the bitchiest

smile Bud had ever seen. She couldn't wait to get a look at the man who'd been taken in by the distraction of full red lips, flashing brown eyes, perfectly even tan skin, and hair so black it almost looked midnight blue.

Again they dutifully followed her around another wing of the house to the other side of the courtyard. She opened the door to a large room with a fireplace, high ceilings, cowhide rugs and plush leather furniture and what was, apparently, a fully stocked bar.

"Since I wasn't expecting you to stay here, the room isn't quite ready. I'll have fresh fruit and flowers sent up in a few minutes. Dinner at eight. My husband will be joining us."

Again, Cann answered on behalf of both of them. "Thank you."

When the door closed, Bud, who was standing in the middle of the room said, "I can't be expected to stay here."

"Why not?" Cann's forehead had formed that wrinkle that he got between his brows when he was concerned about something.

"Because the fresh fruit and flowers haven't been delivered yet."

Cann laughed out loud. "Yeah. The nerve."

"Still. This room is bigger than the house I grew up in."

"Yeah. Me, too."

"So I suppose I could rough it for a couple of nights."

Bud watched Cann's smile creep all the way up and

into his eyes. He was beautiful when he smiled. Well, she thought, he was beautiful all the time, but even more so when he smiled.

As promised, within five minutes there was a knock on the door. One man entered carrying a huge polished wood bowl filled with fruit. A uniformed woman set a tray of assorted cheeses and crackers on the bar while another placed an enormous bouquet of flowers at the other end of the bar.

When they left, Cann looked over at Bud, who said, "That's more like it," just before she ran toward the cheese tray.

"No!" Cann said.

"What?"

"The cheese. It has dairy in it."

"Yeah? Are you prejudiced against Mexican cows or something?"

"No. I'm prejudiced against the Mexican homogenizing process. That cheese may be perfectly safe, but it's not worth takin' a chance. Eat the fruit and the crackers."

She plucked an apple out of the basket. He took it out of her hand, walked to the bar sink, opened one of the bottled waters and used it to wash the apple off. She thought about saying something smart, but was enjoying being cared for too much to spoil it.

"Muchas gracias," she said when he handed her the clean and polished apple.

He chuckled and looked at his watch. "Three hours until dinner. What are you wearing?"

"Oh. I thought I'd go in, let's see… what I have on?"

"Yeah. Same here," he joked.

"You want a toes up?"

"Sure. You know the airplane thing today?" He looked at her and waited. "It was really great."

Cann nodded. It had been great. A real pleasure to see the world from a bird's eye view. "Yeah. It was." He was glad he'd gotten to see that before his demise, which had already been delayed and rescheduled until whenever he got out of prison. He almost laughed out loud at the absurdity of it all.

At precisely eight o'clock Cann and Bud arrived at the bottom of the stairs.

One of the house staff greeted them and showed them to the dining room where Señora Gutierrez was giving direction to someone from the kitchen.

She'd changed into a white gauzy belted dress with a hem that hit at mid-thigh. That was accessorized with a lot of gold jewelry that looked real. A collection of chains from delicate to thick herringbone. Big hoop earrings. And a collection of bangles that clinked together with every move of her wrist.

When she caught sight of Cann, she brightened.

"Come in. Come in." She opened her mouth to say more, but there was a flurry of activity near the front door and some male laughter. They had all three turned toward the sound when the man of the house came hurrying in.

Bud didn't know exactly what she'd expected, but it wasn't anything like Señor Gutierrez. The man was in his early thirties and was giving his wife a run for the money in the beauty department. No wonder she was insecure. He was prettier than she was. At least in Bud's opinion.

"Hola." He went straight to Cann and shook his hand. "Welcome. I'm so glad for the opportunity to do something nice for my friend, Brant Fornight. You can call me Gael." He turned toward Bud and hissed openly. "Madre de dios. Your eyes." He said it reverently as he stared openly. "Such a beautiful and exotic color." Cann wasn't appreciating the adoration and was just about to step in when Gael turned toward him. "Such a lucky man you are."

"Well, I'm not…"

"What's this?" Gael said, looking down at their boots. "Are your shoes wet?"

"Well, we had to cross the river. We were running from Rangers on the other side."

Gael's eyes were dancing with delight. "How romantic!" He looked at Bud.

She shook her head. "No. There was nothing romantic about it."

"Oh," said Gael as if he was disappointed.

Then for the hell of it she added, "Until he picked me up and carried me across so that if they shot at us they'd hit him and not me."

Cann stared at her like she'd lost her mind while Gael threw his head back and laughed. Then he turned to his wife and said, "That is true romance. Don't you agree?"

She sniffed and looked at her nails as if she'd lost interest in the conversation.

"We apologize for our appearance, but we had to run with the clothes on our backs."

Gael turned to the señora with accusation written all over his face. "And you didn't notice that they had nothing with them?" To Cann he said, "My profound apologies. We have failed as your hosts."

"No, really…" Cann began.

"We will rectify this immediately." He turned his head toward the front of the house and shouted, "Juan Ricardo!" They heard footsteps running toward the room. When a man appeared looking eager, if not desperate, to please, Gael said, "Our guests need wardrobes. Send someone to get changes of clothing for Señor Johns. Be sure to include footwear."

Gael looked at Bud. "Your problem is easier to solve. I believe you are the same size as my wife. Please. Consider her wardrobe to be your wardrobe." The señora's eyes were as wide as saucers. He might as well have said he was taking her clothes to the kennel for use by the hunting dogs.

"But…" she began.

"I know you're eager to throw your closet doors wide open to our guest… I'm sorry, did I get your name?"

"Bud."

He stared for a few seconds as if he was waiting to see if she was joking. "I would have expected something magical, intoxicating, enchanting. A name that casts a spell like your eyes. Esmeralda. Tatiana. Ra…"

"Well," Cann interrupted, not liking the tone or direction of the conversation, "it's just plain Bud."

She grinned at Gael. "He calls me sugar."

Cann's eyes went wide just before the WTF lines appeared between his eyebrows.

Gael smiled. "Are you saying I have permission to call you…?"

"No," Cann cut him off before the question was completed. "She's saying you have permission to call her Bud."

Gael chuckled. "Would you like to change or have dinner?" he asked Bud.

"If you can stand to have me sit at the table wearing Super Mercado clothes, I'd like to have dinner."

Their host smiled like he was genuinely enjoying himself.

Over dinner, which was roasted flank steak and grilled vegetables, they explained why they were running from the Texas Rangers.

Gael had looked more and more serious as the tale had taken shape. "You are not outlaws, my friends. You are saints." He glanced at his wife. "We have not been fortunate enough to have little ones yet, but I look forward to the day."

"Well, now that we've told our story," Cann said, "maybe you'll tell us how you got to be good friends with Brant."

Gael sat back and smiled. "I cannot share details, but I'll tell you that he was key in assisting with an entanglement at the capital of the great state of Texas." Cann nodded and sat back. Gael got to his feet. "Please forgive me, friends, but my business sometimes requires evening hours. For the next two days, please, how do you say it? Make yourself at home?"

"Yeah. Make yourself at home. Thanks. That's very nice of you," Cann said.

"We have a heated pool and a kitchen staff capable of making anything you wish at any time of day." He looked at Bud. "Be sure to make a stop by my wife's closet on your way up."

Bud looked at Señora Gutierrez and knew she was going to thoroughly enjoy that.

When Señora Gutierrez opened her closet door, Bud walked in and said, "Wow. Did you know there's a boutique next door? That must be really convenient." The sarcasm apparently escaped Señora Gutierrez along with the underlying humor. "Well, I'm not going to bother to ask what you *do*. It's pretty clear that you're a professional shopper."

"Image is everything to a woman in my position."

"Really? What position is that?"

The woman's stony expression indicated that chat time was over.

The closet was about the same size as a starter apartment. It even had three rooms complete with drawered islands and upholstered benches, presumably for putting on silk stockings or taking off boots.

Señora Gutierrez stood at the doorway and glared as Bud walked through the closet. After surveying racks of hanging dresses and suits, Bud finally asked, "Don't you own any jeans?"

Without a word, Señora Gutierrez walked to one of the larger island drawers, pulled it out, and motioned palm up like a game show hostess.

Bud pulled out the top pair that were pressed and folded as if they were on display in a store. They were denimish, but they were more like leggings than pants. "Hmmm. Always wondered what I'd look like in these." She smiled at Señora Gutierrez. "I'll take them. Thank you."

That was what some would call the 'foundation' piece of Bud's spree. After being directed to the underthings column of drawers, Bud thought she might have died and gone to heaven. She'd known that beautiful lingerie existed because she'd seen it in photos and video. What she hadn't known was that it could feel as luxuriously silky as recently washed and conditioned hair. Plus, the lace and other embellishments such as hand embroidery could make a two hundred dollar pair of panties a work of art.

"Great heavenly days," she said, holding up a pair of sapphire blue panties and bra to match.

She nabbed two other underwear sets while she was there, after which the señora said, pointedly, "Please keep those as a gift. Return will not be necessary."

Bud didn't dignify the inference with a response.

After plundering through shoes, Bud chose two pairs of sandals, one pair of three-inch block heels, and one pair of flats, and some highly polished leather ankle boots.

After draping a violet-colored silk nightshirt over her arm, she walked slowly along double rows of hanging shirts, blouses, and tops. She stopped next to a rose tunic with three-quarter sleeves and a deep vee neck. Enough coverage to pass the modesty test, but still sexy.

Bud ran her hand down the length of the sleeve. When she felt the softness of the material, she knew it was *the* one. She didn't feel the least bit bad about sampling the wardrobe. The señora would never miss the few things she'd claimed.

However, when she began to take the tunic off its hanger, Señora Gutierrez cleared her throat and said, "That is one of my favorites. How about this one?" She pulled out two other tunics.

Bud shook her head and said, "No, thank you. I like this one." Señora Gutierrez glared. "And tu closet es mi closet," she said sweetly. She punctuated that by batting her eyelashes exactly the way Señora Gutierrez had done with Cann.

The woman's eyes flashed as if she might have a full-blown tamale tantrum, but she managed to restrain herself.

"Swimsuits?" Bud asked.

Señora Gutierrez huffed, stomped toward a drawer

and, in her eagerness to please, pulled the entire drawer out of its shelf so that drawer and contents spilled onto the floor.

"Oh, gracias," Bud said with her best fake sincerity. "It's so easy for me to see them all this way."

The señora backed away, recognizing for the first time that perhaps Bud wasn't as devoid of power and ripe for manipulation as she'd seemed on first impression.

Bud plucked a blood-red one piece from the floor. It had cutouts on the sides so that it was almost as revealing as a bikini, but the center panel hid her belly button. The pregnancy wasn't showing, but she was feeling hyperaware regardless.

Gathering her armload of treasure, she started toward the door saying, "I know the way."

Cann was sitting on one of the tuxedo Chesterfields reading. He looked up as she entered and shut the door behind her with her foot. Seeing the load of girlie stuff she was carrying, he said, "Have a nice time?"

"Oh my God, Johns," she said with heightened color in her cheeks, eyes shining like she'd won the lottery. "The woman has a closet as big as this ginormous room! It's… It's…"

"Obscene?"

"Yes! Obscene! Which is one of the reasons why I had such fun relieving her of some of the burden of…um…"

"Obscenity?"

"Yes! Exactly! I have to go hang these up. Or try them on."

He chuckled because she was practically jumping up and down.

A fleeting thought of Molly danced across his mind. He knew she'd liked clothes, as all women do, and wondered if she would have reacted the same way if she'd been given access to outfits that cost more than an average mortgage payment. Oddly, the thought of Molly didn't sting and send him straight to the bar for a whiskey. Instead, the thought lit on his consciousness like a butterfly. A pleasant memory that danced across the screen of his mind long enough to be appreciated and cherished, then disappeared into the recesses of memory.

There was a knock around ten o'clock. When Cann answered, two men entered smiling and nodding. One carried folded clothing and two shoe boxes. The other carried clothes on hangers. They walked straight back to the dressing area and opened the closet.

Bud, who had spent an hour and a half in a leisurely hot bath, chose that time to open the bathroom door wearing the newly acquired night shirt and no bra. "Johns, did you hear someone at the…?" She took one look at the two men about to put clothes away in the closet, shrieked a little, "Eep," and disappeared into the bath again.

Cann took in a big breath, let it out again, and said, "Jesus."

When they left, he knocked on the bath door. "You can come out. They're gone."

She opened the door. "What were they doing? Bringing you clothes? How did they find all those clothes at this time of night? It would have to be some kind of specialty store because there aren't a lot of people your size down here. You know?"

Cann hadn't heard a thing she'd said. He'd been too busy staring at the way her nipples prodded the silk shirt.

"Johns? Are you staring at my…?"

His eyes jerked up to hers, which stood out like neon because of the lavender color of the shirt. That was when he knew he might be in actual trouble.

He swallowed and pulled his gaze away. "They brought clothes."

"I know. That's what I said." Her tone was dry and full of mock patience. "Let's see what they brought you."

"Well, maybe you want to put on…"

"Wow. These shirts are gorgeous, Johns. You're going to be beautiful in this one." The sentence he'd been forming froze in his mind when Bud speculated that he might be beautiful. "Look! They found you new biker boots. Only these are better than the ones you ruined."

"We ruined."

"Whatever. We're going to look like respectable people."

"The main thing is that we *are* respectable people," Cann said. The smile she gave Cann in return was so dazzling he turned away for fear of blushing. "You can take the bed closest to the bathroom."

"Okay. I guess you can have the other one."

He didn't turn around, but she heard him snort softly.

CHAPTER EIGHT

"Brant." It was a statement of fact. Texas Ranger, Forge Russell, had been told that Brant was on the line.

"Russ. Like to buy you a taco. Sit down of a sensitive nature."

"Where? When?"

"You know the truck by the river. One?"

After a brief pause, Russell said, "I'll be there."

"By yourself."

"That sensitive, huh?"

"Your ears only."

"Alright then. I'll manage it."

Russ ordered four tacos and a half-sized bottle of Dos Equis.

"You drinkin' on the job?" Brant asked.

Russ gave him a look. "Somebody don't like it. They can call the Rangers."

Brant laughed and shook his head. "Yeah. Like that's happenin'."

They sat down on the picnic bench furthest away

from the truck and other benches. If they talked in conversational tones, it would be private enough.

"This about your boy?" Russell asked. Brant nodded as he took half a taco in a single bite. "Heard he went across even with shots fired in the air and orders to stop. Left a dually in the middle of the river, but when we went back to fish it out and get the VIN, it was gone."

"Imagine that." Brant chuckled as he finished chewing and swallowed. "We need to manage gettin' him back in, Russ."

"What're you askin', Brant?"

"I want you to go on down to Del Rio and be the one to take him into custody. You put him someplace safe while we handle the legal side of it."

"Brant, I don't get to pick and choose my assignments like I was the goddamn president of a goddamn motorcycle club."

Brant nodded. "You've collected favors just like me. I'm callin' one in. You do the same."

"It's that important."

"I'm sayin' so."

Russell was quiet for a couple of minutes while he ate. "This here is good food."

"Always has been."

"So happens I might have somethin' to call in."

"Thought you might."

"But it'd mean I might call on you one of these days."

"Not goin' anywhere."

"Okay then. It's about a four hour drive down there. What time do you want him to come across?"

"Noon."

"The girl's father has to be informed. He'll be there."

"After tonight at midnight, she can make her own decisions. Garland and I'll be there in case she doesn't want to go home with him." Russell nodded. "Gonna be TV cameras."

Russell's head jerked up. "Why's that?"

"The so-called 'kidnapping' has been all over the news for a week. It's only fair the story be set right. My boy's a champion of the unborn. Hero to millions of true believers."

"Christ, Brant."

"Just lettin' you know to shave extra close. Margie'll want you to look your best."

"You're the devil."

"Been called worse."

CHAPTER NINE

For the first time since they'd been traveling together, Bud woke first.

After her morning bathroom routine, she had a look through the clothes that were delivered for Cann. She found what she was looking for and did a two-second victory dance.

Six minutes later she was shoving Cann's shoulder.

"Come on. Get up. We've got things to do." He rumbled in an atavistic way that brought to mind the image of waking a grizzly from hibernation. "Wakey. Wakey."

He opened his eyes and blinked three times before saying, in a voice that was rough and deep from sleep, "What are you wearin'?"

Bud looked down at her body like she forgot. "It's a swimsuit."

"Jesus."

"Look!" She held up swim trunks. "Put these on. We're goin' swimmin'."

"No."

"Yes."

FIFTEEN MINUTES LATER they were at the bottom of the grand staircase. Cann was wearing a long sleeve tee over his swim trunks that came to the knee. Bud was wearing her night shirt. That had been a whole other conversation.

"Why are you wearin' your pajama top to go swimmin'?"

"This shirt is very versatile. Last night it was a sleep shirt. This morning it's a bathing suit cover up."

He laughed. "I don't think so. For somethin' to be a 'cover up' it has to cover somethin' up and that thing isn't hidin' anythin'."

She threw her head back so that, when she looked up at him, it was like looking down her nose. "You're missing the point, caveman. The purpose isn't to be a burqa. It's supposed to be a suggestion of feminine mystique."

He laughed harder. "Feminine mystique?"

THE MAN WHOSE uniform distinguished him from other household staff; he wore a vest over a white shirt with dark pants and the look screamed for a name tag, approached them.

"Buenos dias. Desayuno?"

In Spanish Cann told him that they'd like to go for a swim. The man said that the mistress of the house would be out most of the day. He asked if they'd like to have breakfast in the solarium by the pool. Cann said that would be nice if it wasn't too much trouble. He told the man what he'd like and gave instructions to bring the lady fruit, bottled water, and steak grilled well done.

The man, who apparently ran the household, motioned to a boy dressed in white shirt, dark pants, no vest and asked him to show the guests to the solarium.

After walking around two sides of the house, they arrived at the solarium. After stepping inside Cann and Bud both stopped to stare.

The room was mostly glass looking out onto gardens. Inside, tropical plants thrived in dirt beds with specialized irrigation systems.

The interior wall featured a huge cage, forty feet long, six feet wide and sixteen feet high. The floor was made of pea gravel with a large drain in the center. Four fifteen-foot trees with large dark green, waxy leaves were planted in a row.

Inside the cage were a dozen brightly colored parakeets. Their chirps echoed throughout the room, infusing the space with life and cheer so that it was almost impossible not to smile.

The pool was large, perhaps a third of Olympic size, and clear as bathtub water. In short, the room was breathtaking.

"Jesus," said Cann.

Bud grinned at him, pulled off her 'cover up', letting it fall where it landed, and ran for the pool like a little kid. Cann waited until she surfaced. She popped up from the water like a cork.

"Whoa," she yelled. "It's amazing! Stop standing

there like an old man. Come in."

He walked over to the white cast iron table. It was surrounded by six chairs with cushions covered in red with thin gold stripes. After pulling the tee over his head and draping it over the back of a chair, he turned and aimed a cannonball close enough to where Bud was treading water to create a wave.

When he came up above water, Bud was laughing. They swam and splashed for a while, both forgetting their troubles as if they'd been washed away by luxurious pool water.

Cann noticed the door opening. One of the staff held it while the butler wheeled a cart in.

"Chow's up," Cann said to Bud.

"We're havin' breakfast? In here?"

"That's the plan."

"You know, Johns, this might be the best day of my life."

"That's not sayin' much, sugar. You're still a kid."

"For fifteen more hours. If you call me a kid again after that, you will be bopped."

He laughed. "Bopped?"

"You know what I mean."

He shook his head. "I don't."

"Well, call me a kid tomorrow and you'll find out."

He knew she wasn't a kid on the inside whether it was that day or the next, but he took a perverse pleasure in seeing the fire light behind her eyes.

When they climbed the steps to exit the pool, two

staff members rushed forward with thick white terry robes. One small. One extra large.

"Gracias," Bud said, smiling at Cann like she'd become bilingual.

They sat down in front of a breakfast fit for European monarchy.

"Steak!" Bud said. "I've got steak!"

"I know," Cann said.

"I love steak," she continued. "Maybe not quite so done, but still…"

"The extra grilling's a precaution. Just to make sure you don't pick up anything that would make you sick."

"Right." She peeled an orange and found that the flesh inside was bright red. After popping a section in her mouth, she hummed then said, "This is beautiful and good. So good." She looked at the pool, the thick white robe, and at Cann who had lifted a glass with red juice and leafy celery sticks, "Is that what I think it is?"

"Bloody Mary."

"Oh. My. God."

Cann chuckled and nodded. "I know. Life is strange."

"It's like that book, you know, *The Secret*?"

He shook his head. "No. I don't know."

"Well, it says if you say what you want in the right way at the right time, it'll happen."

Cann put down his glass and stared at her for a few beats before saying, "I don't want to spend more than three nights in jail for this."

"I want to find a way to go back to school after the

baby is born."

"I want to find the guy who killed my family."

"I want my baby to always be safe."

"I want your baby to always be safe."

She looked around. "Did you ever dream about a life like this? I mean, you know, seriously?"

He followed suit and looked around before answering. "Honestly, no. I guess I'm kind of a simple guy." He looked over at her. "You?"

She shook her head. "This was fun. Today. But I don't see myself livin' like this."

"I guess city planners travel a lot."

"Yeah." She smiled. "I don't know about that. What I do know is that I'm not makin' plans for just me anymore. Got somebody else to think about."

He nodded thoughtfully. "Kids need to stay in the same place."

"They do." She nodded. "School and all. Maybe I'll make enough money to have a nanny. So I could be gone for a couple of days now and then."

AFTER MORE SWIMMING and lunch, Bud and Cann explored the house and found the media room, which was complete with an enormous library of DVDs in both Spanish and English. He chose *No Mercy*. She chose *A Walk in the Clouds*. As they were leaving, the butler intercepted them.

In Spanish he told Cann that dinner would be at eight then disappeared.

"Dinner's at eight," he told Bud. "We should work on your Spanish."

She yawned. "I was thinking naps. I've got time, right?"

He looked at his watch. "Yes. You've got time."

SHE NAPPED FOR almost two hours while Cann sat on one of the Chesterfields and read.

"You don't have to babysit me," she'd said, when she lay down.

"I'm not leavin' you alone here."

He said it matter-of-factly as if the thought was out of the question. And she reminded herself again not to get too used to that. It mimicked devotion, but wasn't. He was just a nice guy doing a good deed. That was all.

BUD STOOD IN front of the gigantic bathroom mirror blowing her hair dry, wearing the sapphire panties and bra that felt like they were made in heaven. When she pulled the skinny jeans on, she thought, "Damn. These look good. And I'll probably only be able to wear them for another month."

She sighed, stepped into the high-heeled sandals, and pulled the tunic over her head. It fell to mid-thigh, but draped her body in the most luscious way. She was pretty sure she'd never looked so good. Ever.

When she stepped out, Cann scanned her down and up, then shook his head. "Jesus."

She took that as confirmation that she'd never looked

so good. Ever.

As he opened the door to the hallway, he said, "What do you want for your birthday? I hear it's a special one."

"It is. Age of majority. I'm getting what I want."

"What's that?"

"Freedom."

Cann had to admire the commitment she'd brought to finding her own way at any cost. Looking into her face was like meeting hope. She was the essence of optimism, believing that the future held good and marvelous things, adventures for the taking. She was the very opposite of him; a soul withered by sorrow and loss with nothing to look forward to except death, embittered by hatred of the faceless someone who'd brought complete devastation and destruction to his world.

DINNER CONVERSATION WAS mostly about the drug war zone since their hosts lived within a few miles of the Texas border. It was awkward in the sense that, for the second night in a row, Gael ignored his wife while she behaved as if there was nothing at all unusual about that.

A couple of times Bud had caught her hostess eyeing the rose tunic. "I will leave this behind when I leave tomorrow," she said.

Señora Gutierrez took a sip of wine from her goblet then said, "Of course not. It will be my honor for you to keep it. I can always get another."

Perhaps there was a dig in that last thought, but Bud was finding it harder to hate the señora, seeing that she had a lavish lifestyle, but without her husband's love or even respect.

After dessert, Gael Gutierrez turned to Cann and said, "I've heard from Brant. He would like to discuss the plans for tomorrow. In my study there is a worry-free landline. You are welcome to make the call there and chat while the ladies and I enjoy coffee."

"Thank you." Cann nodded to Bud before following Gael out of the room.

After a few minutes of awkward silence during which Bud found the pouring of coffee fascinating, Gael returned and entertained her with stories of his adventures in the wilds of Argentina when he was her age.

"WHEN YOU COME back across they're going to grab you, but the guy who'll take you into custody is a friend of mine. Likewise, the federale who will walk you across is a friend of Gael's. You're in good hands."

"Bud…" Cann began. His first thought was to be scared for what would happen to her. Where would she sleep? Would she eat right?

"That's the last thing you've got to worry about. Garland and I will be there to get her and bring her home. We'll take care of her until you're back." He chuckled. "Garland's already made her an appointment with the best obstetrician in Austin." Brant paused. "You won't be gone long. We're lawyered up in ways you can't imagine. If necessary we'll tap Brand's resources and you can't begin to imagine how deep and wide that goes. Plus, this is a sympathetic situation to a hell of a lot of people. You'll be a hero to them."

"Jesus."

"Yeah. Exactly. News people will be there so have that girl dress like a Madonna. Modest. Girl next door."

"That *is* who she is."

"Then that'll come across and people'll be on your side. Havin' the public on your side, well, it's powerful. Don't worry. You did a good thing. It was a stupid thing, but it was also good and you're not gonna suffer for it if we can help it."

"Thanks, boss."

THEY SAT ON the sides of their respective beds, facing each other.

"When?" Bud said.

"Noon. Brant says for you to wear somethin' nice. There'll be TV cameras and he thinks the impression is important. Modest young mother-to-be."

"What's gonna happen?"

"They're gonna take me into custody at the border."

All of a sudden the full-blown reality hit Bud. She wondered where her head had been. Hadn't she known that was what was going to happen? Cann had told her often enough.

"No." She shook her head as her eyes filled with tears. She practically threw herself across the few feet that separated them and, before Cann knew what had happened, she was straddling him with her face buried in his neck, sobbing. Instinctively he put his arms around her.

"Shhh. It's gonna be okay. Brant is gonna get me out."

"When?"

"I don't know when."

She drew back and looked at him with puffy eyes that broke his heart and he realized that, sometime between the Mountain Dew vending machine and that moment, she'd started caring about what happened to him. "No more than three nights."

HE SMILED, REACHING up to wipe tears away with his thumb. "Yeah. No more than three nights." He stood up and set her on her feet. "You need to get a good night's rest. Tomorrow's gonna bring a lot of havoc."

He realized that he'd started caring about what happened to her as well. The last thing he'd intended was for the girl to get attached to a walking dead man.

She'd already had some rough breaks. Her mama died when she was too young to remember. Her old man had abdicated his role as parent. Her boyfriend had knocked her up and abandoned her. And, Christ, she was stuck with the name 'Bud'.

It really wouldn't be fair for her to grieve for him when he was gone. That was not what he wanted. The whole point was leaving nobody behind who cared one way or the other. Seemed like he'd fucked that up without intending to.

THE NEXT MORNING, when she came out of the bathroom,

Cann was sitting there with a huge chocolate cupcake featuring a lit pink candle. Bud's eyes lit with delight and darted between Cann and the cupcake and back again.

"Please don't make me sing. 'Cause I can't. But Happy birthday."

Bud's eyes were still a little swollen from all the crying the night before, but that didn't mean that there weren't more tears.

Cann was baffled. "Hey. Hey. What's the matter?"

"I never had a birthday cake before," she sniffled.

And his heart hurt for her even more. He wanted to punch her old man in the face and rearrange his nose.

"Well, here's what you do. You make a wish." She opened her mouth. "No. Wait. You don't tell. Anybody. You keep it to yourself. And then you blow out the candle. Better hurry 'cause it's almost gone."

She closed her eyes briefly then opened them and blew out the candle. Without warning she grabbed his face and pulled him down so she could plant a big kiss on his cheek. "Thank you, Johns. You're the best."

"You're welcome, sugar. But don't be making me bigger than life."

"I can't make you bigger than life, Johns. You made yourself bigger than life."

"Jesus." He scrubbed a big hand over his face. "You need to get some breakfast and go pick out some clothes."

"I'm havin' cupcake for breakfast."

"No. You are not. The cupcake isn't to eat. It's not safe. It was just like a… a prop."

She went for it, but he was faster. He held it above his head while he walked backwards toward the window with her jumping for it the whole way and him laughing at her.

When he turned the window crank with one hand, she said, "You will not throw my cupcake out!"

"No?" he said, grinning.

"No!"

He threw the cupcake out.

She looked out. There it was. Her beautiful cupcake on the grass below. One of the guards holding an automatic weapon was looking up with open curiosity.

She turned on Cann. "I hate you."

As she stomped off to go find clothes to wear, he laughed, "Is it the pregnancy hormones? I thought I was bigger than life."

"You are. You're the biggest asshole I know. I wanted that cupcake."

"Darlin'. When you get across the border, Brant'll get you all the cupcakes you can eat."

She narrowed her eyes. "So we're at darlin' again?"

Cann's smile gradually disappeared. "We should have been at darlin' all along."

Bud's face fell because she understood what he was trying to say. He was sorry that she cared about him.

CHAPTER TEN

B UD WAS STANDING in the middle of her hostess's closet trying to decide what to wear to the epic walk across the border. She pulled out a few things, but nothing seemed just right. She wanted sedate, but it was her eighteenth birthday and she didn't want to dress like she was forty-five.

Perhaps the late October day was cool somewhere, but it was hot in Del Rio. She was lost in indecision and running out of time to decide. Out of the corner of her eye she saw one of the maids pass by the closet door.

Bud stepped to the entrance and said, "Can you come help me please?" The maid, who was straightening pillows, looked around as if Bud might be addressing someone else. "Yes. You. Come." Bud made a gesture with her hand.

It took some doing to coax the young woman to sit down on the bench Bud was pointing to, but she finally relented and did so. Bud quickly acted out what she wanted, by holding outfits up and saying, "Si o no?"

The maid said no to the first three outfits, but smiled and nodded yes to the plain tan linen dress that fell just above the knee. It had a modest scoop neck, three-quarter sleeves, and looked great with the high-heeled sandals. The maid rose, opened one of the cupboards and pulled out a big brown Brahmin bag.

When Bud saw it, she nodded and giggled. It was big enough to carry everything she was taking with her and would look stylish, too.

"Gracias," Bud said.

The maid smiled and seemed as pleased as Bud was.

CANN WAS WAITING when she finished getting ready and emerged from the bathroom.

His eyes swept her figure appreciatively. "Jesus. You look good."

Unused to compliments like that, she flushed slightly. "Thank you."

"Ready?"

"I guess."

Gael was waiting at the front door. "You look lovely," he said. "The car is waiting."

It took only twenty minutes to drive to the border crossing. Gael was on the phone with Brant.

"Here," Cann said to Bud as she sat next to him in the backseat. "You take the money." He handed her all the cash that was left. "Brant and Garland, that's his wife, are gonna take care of you. So don't worry."

"What do you mean?"

"I mean they're gonna make sure you have a place to stay, doctor appointments, maybe help you find a job.

Stuff like that. The details aren't important. What is important is that you and that baby are not gonna be on the street again. You understand?"

Her eyes were large and liquid. She nodded as a single tear spilled onto her cheek.

"No. No. No. No. Not this again," Cann said. "It shouldn't make you sad that you're gonna be okay."

"That doesn't make me sad, Johns. It's that I don't know what's gonna happen to you next."

"I'll be fine. You need to show those TV fucks that you're no little girl."

She nodded and smiled as she turned her attention to pulling herself together.

They parked a short distance from the bridge and got out of the car.

Bud turned to Gael. "Thank you for everything you've done for us."

He showed Bud his beautifully white straight teeth when he smiled. "It was delightful. You're welcome anytime."

A uniformed officer approached, shook hands with Gael and said something to Cann in Spanish. As they walked away, Bud heard Gael telling someone on the phone, in English, that the transfer had begun.

They could hear the noise of a large crowd and see that people were lining the roads on the other side.

"What is that about?" she said to Cann.

"Don't know," he replied.

The federale walking next to Cann said, "They're here for you."

"Me?"

The man glanced back at Bud. "And her."

The minute they stepped onto U.S. soil, Russell stepped in front of Cann. "Put your wrists together." Cann complied. Russell snapped handcuffs on him and said, "This isn't procedure, as I'm sure you know, but you're comin' voluntarily. Right?"

"Yeah," Cann said. "Voluntarily."

TV reporters and cameras tried to get close. The three Rangers with Russell kept them at a reasonable distance, but they shouted questions at Cann.

"Cannon! What do you have to say to your fans?"

Cann looked at Russell, bewildered. "Fans?"

A faint smile traced Russell's mouth as he shook his head. "Thought I'd seen it all, son. But this is a first for me, too."

Cann turned to see Bud swarmed by reporters. He found Brant in the crowd and saw that he was seconds away from shoving people out of the way and rescuing her.

Bud never took her eyes off Cann. Just before he was put in the Ranger SUV he said, "Don't worry."

She couldn't hear him, but she knew what he said. She held up three fingers. When he realized what she meant, he grinned.

The reporter closest to Bud put a microphone next to her face and said, "People are eager to hear your story.

What do you have to say?"

Her father reached her before Brant. He stepped in front of the mic and said, "She doesn't have anything to say. Now get out of the way and let us pass." He grabbed Bud's elbow, but she jerked it away.

"Don't touch me. And don't speak for me either." She turned to the reporter who asked the question. "This is my father. He planned to have my baby aborted against my will. So I ran and the angels were smiling when a stranger named Cannon Johns found me. When he heard my story, he helped me get away until I turned eighteen. Today. He helped me save the life of my baby, knowing the risk."

"So Cannon Johns is not the father of your baby?"

She shook her head. "No. He's not my lover. But he is my hero. And he's not the one who should be in jail. It's my daddy who ought to be in jail."

Everyone present turned in unison to register the look of shock on the Ranger's face at being publicly called out by his daughter.

Then Bud saw Brant elbowing his way through the people like a linebacker. As soon as he was within reach, she stretched out her hand so he could pull her to him. He put a big arm around her shoulders and slowly began to move her through the throng.

Pro Life advocates lined the road, most carrying signs. She heard constant shouts of, "God Bless You".

It took almost half an hour to make their way to where Garland waited. She sat waiting patiently behind the wheel, but wore lines of concern on her face. Brant put Bud in the front passenger seat next to his wife and got in back. And even then, the crowd didn't want to let the car go.

Little by little Garland ooched forward, eager to leave, but not wanting injury on her conscience.

When they were finally clear, Garland turned to Bud and said, "I'm Garland. Happy birthday."

"Doesn't feel happy."

"Well, it should." Garland smiled. "You're baking the best kind of baby. The kind that's really, really wanted. By the way, I like your bag."

Without hesitation Bud said, "You can have it. It's the least I can do. Since you picked me up and all."

Garland was so touched she was speechless. She assumed the girl didn't know that the car's driver was one of the richest women in the world. "That is very generous of you, but I think you need a bag of your own." She smiled. "Brant will buy me one, won't you?"

Brant huffed. "Jesus."

Bud swiveled in her seat belt so that she could see Brant in the backseat. "Is that every biker's favorite word?"

He chuckled. "I don't know. Maybe."

"Well, either you're a seriously religious bunch or you're in trouble for… I forgot what they call it."

"Blasphemy?" Garland supplied.

"Yeah. Blasphemy." She faced forward again. "I'm worried about Johns."

"You call him Johns?" Brant asked from the backseat. She nodded, but didn't answer. "So, if I understand the situation correctly, you're homeless, jobless, got no prospects, but you're worried about Cann?"

"He's the one in handcuffs. I'm the one in the cushy car on her way to lunch."

"We didn't have lunch either," Garland said. "What're we having?"

Brant pulled out his phone. "We can stop in Uvalde."

"How far is that?" Bud asked.

"'Bout an hour. The way my wife drives it might be forty-five minutes."

"There's a place on the way called Lunker's Grill. Burgers. Chicken fried steak. How's that sound?"

"Burger. Yes! Cann wouldn't let me eat anything good since we crossed into Mexico. He kept going, 'That's not safe. That's not safe either'. He wouldn't even let me have my birthday cupcake."

After a pregnant pause, Brant said, "Cann got you a birthday cupcake?"

Garland caught Brant's gaze in the rearview mirror and the two of them exchanged a look.

"Did you make a wish?" Garland asked.

Bud smiled. "Oh, yeah. I wished that he wouldn't have to spend more than three nights in jail."

"Why three nights? Why not one or five? Or none?" Garland asked.

Bud related the whole story about the pool, the bathrobe, the Bloody Mary, and *The Secret*.

"And he said, 'I don't want to spend more than three nights in jail'."

Garland looked at Brant in the rearview mirror again. He knew that look.

Brant pressed Brash's contact number.

"What's happenin'?" said Brash when he saw it was his dad calling.

"Got the package. Russ has got Cann. Want you to find out which federal judge he'll be in front of. See if you can pinpoint his heart's desire."

Brash grinned into the phone. "I will, but there're already a whole bunch of powerful reasons for the judge to see things our way."

"What do you mean?"

"Pro Lifers all over the news. They're gathering outside District Court and over at the capitol, too. Demanding Cann's release. Never saw anything like it. All these church folk demandin' release of a biker?" He laughed. "You gotta admit it's a twist of fate."

"That it is."

"Preachers are down there with 'em. They've been interviewed by the local news stations. All say the same thing. That we ought to be erecting a statue of Cannon Johns, not puttin' him in cuffs."

"Hmm," Brant grunted. "Couldn't hurt to grease the judge anyway. I like insurance."

"Yeah. Those guys, the fed judges, are more prickly than usual, since they're appointed and all."

"You know how to get around that."

"Indeed I do."

"Keep me posted."

"Hey. You probably didn't see yourself on the news."

"No," Brant said slowly. "I think I'd hoped to make it safely to death without ever hearing those words."

Brash laughed. "That little girl did us proud. Said Cann is a hero who helped a stranger, at great risk to himself."

"She said that?"

"Yeah."

"Jesus." Garland and Bud, who were eavesdropping, exchanged a glance. "We need to try to get him out of there before he spends a fourth night in jail."

"What? Why that in particular?"

"Superstition."

"Whatever."

"Yeah. Make sure everything else is good to go. Like we talked about."

"On it."

Brant ended the call. "Garland. Stop drivin' like an old lady. We're hungry."

"I can't drive fast and listen in on your calls at the same time," Garland insisted with a touch of aggravation.

Brant snorted. "Brash says folks are gatherin' outside the District Court and on the capitol grounds with signs. The evangelicals want Cann released."

Bud perked up at that. "You think they'll have some influence?"

Brant grinned. "Oh yeah. The law serves the people,

not the other way around. If the people make it clear that justice will be best served by releasing Cann, that's what'll happen." He turned away and muttered, "One way or the other."

"What was that?" Bud asked.

"We'll get it done. Don't worry."

"That's what Cann kept saying. 'Don't worry'."

"Well, bikers like to keep our women stress-free," Brant said.

Garland laughed so hard at that she almost guffawed.

When her amusement died, Bud said, "I'm not a biker's woman."

Brant nodded in what might have appeared to be agreement to anyone except Garland. She wasn't fooled and made that clear by giving him a knowing look in the rearview mirror.

When they walked into Lunker's Grill, several patrons did double takes and stared as Brant, Garland, and Bud were led to a table. Brant vetoed the first suggestion and asked for the booth in the far corner. He stood by the side against the wall until Garland slid in, then sat so that he was on the outside and had a view of the entire establishment. Bud had the other side all to herself.

The waitress brought menus and said she'd be right back with water.

When she returned she said, "You folks have had quite a day. We're honored to have you here." She looked at Bud. "What can I get you?"

"I want a hamburger with everything."

"Cheese?"

"Yeah."

"French fries?"

"Yeah. Lots."

The waitress chuckled. "Okay. Lots."

She turned to Brant and Garland who said, "We're havin' what she's havin'."

"And a Coke," Bud added.

"Three Cokes," Brant said.

When the waitress was gone, Brant said, "We've got a couple of things we'd like to discuss with you."

Bud glanced to Garland and back to Brant. "Okay."

"The club would like to make you an offer of employment." Bud blinked twice and took a deep breath. "We have members who live at the club and others who have their own place, but stay sometimes. We keep somebody on who tends the bar and keeps it stocked, tidies up, does the grocery shopping and cooks meals a couple of times a day. Our girl who's been doin' the job is takin' off. She got sweet on a biker from Tucson and he's makin' her his old lady. As it happens, Cann told me you have the skills that match the job requirements. You know how to cook and clean up."

Bud was near dumbstruck. She'd been trying not to think too hard about what was going to happen when she got to Austin. She had eight hundred dollars and some pesos to exchange, but she knew she had to get a job that would issue a paycheck soon. What Brant was saying sounded like manna from heaven.

"I, um, don't know how to bartend, but I can figure it out."

Brant gave her a warm, fatherly smile. "I have no doubt of that.

"The job doesn't pay six figures and there's not much down time, but it comes with a room, a scholarship, and people who'll care what happens to you."

For a minute she was afraid she'd suffered a brain blip.

"A place to stay?" she croaked.

"Yeah. And when you get ready to go back to school, the club will pick up the tab and make sure you have time to go to class."

She took a big breath. "That's…" She couldn't really find the words. It wasn't just an offer she couldn't refuse. It was everything in the world that she and the baby needed. A job. A place to stay. Maybe the safest place anywhere. And a chance to go to school.

Garland reached over and squeezed her hand. "He forgot to tell you that it includes health benefits. I've already made an appointment for you to visit the obstetrician tomorrow. I'll take you myself. If you want to accept what the club is offering, that is."

Bud was still speechless, but nodding her head. She felt overwhelmed, like she'd cry if she tried to make a sound.

The waitress arrived with their burgers.

"Wow," said Garland. "How did you get these done

so fast?"

"Oh," said the waitress, "this time of day we've always got meat on the griddle and fries in the basket. Somebody always comes through that door who wants what we're sellin'."

"Smells wonderful," said Garland, nabbing a fry. When she realized Bud wasn't eating, she said, "What's wrong?"

"I just… I'm not sure how to thank you."

"Now listen here," said Brant. "You don't need to thank us. Once you start dealin' with my boys you may decide that cussin' me out is more appropriate." He took a bite, started to chew and said, "Um." He looked at Garland. "Good stuff."

She nodded her agreement.

"You'll have to learn to stand up to the men, but somehow I don't think that's gonna be a problem for you, darlin'."

She smirked at the use of darlin'. "I'll do my best, um…"

"Call me Brant." He looked at his wife. "You can call her Your Highness."

Garland slapped his arm playfully. "Garland. Please."

Bud popped a French fry in her mouth, chewed, swallowed, then said, "Does, um, Johns live at the club?"

Brant and Garland both heard the underlying sentiment in that innocent question. It wasn't unusual for teens to have crushes on good-looking bikers, but Brant and Garland both, privately, thought it was more. The longing of a person who might be mature beyond her years.

"He's been away a long time," Brant started slowly. "Had some heartache."

"I know," Bud said.

"He told you?" Brant sounded surprised.

"Yes." Bud nodded and Brant's gaze flicked to Garland.

"Well, he's been gone a long time and he doesn't have a place of his own. So, yeah, when we get him out, he'll be at the club. For now. Cann requires what you might call special handling."

"I know." She looked up at Brant. "I'm really grateful…"

"Now I already told you, there's no need for all that. It's simple. We got a job and a place to stay. You need a job and a place to stay. After a week, you may decide you'd rather take your chances elsewhere."

"No." She shook her head. "I can recognize a bird nest on the ground."

Brant treated her to a lopsided grin that let her know he'd been a heartbreaker sometime before she was born. "That's commendable. Not everybody knows when to grab what's right in front of them. Cann said you're a worthy girl."

"He did?" Garland had to smother her laughter at the eagerness in Bud's tone.

"Yeah," said Brant. "Don't read too much into it. Like I said, special handlin'."

"You think they're gonna let him go?" Bud asked.

Brant nodded. "Oh, yeah. I know it. Maybe not today or tomorrow, but…"

"The next day," she put in. "Three days. That's what he said."

"If I understand the story the way you told it, that wasn't a promise. It was a wish."

"Same thing."

Brant shook his head. "No the hell it's not…"

Garland put her hand on Brant's forearm to stop him. "Maybe it is and maybe it isn't for her. Let her live her life and find her own way. In good time she'll either prove that up or adopt another view."

He smiled at his wife. "When did you get to be a font of sage wisdom?"

"I always have been and if you don't know that, you haven't been paying attention." Garland winked at Bud.

Brant scoffed at his burger basket and took another enormous bite.

CHAPTER ELEVEN

It was about four o'clock when they pulled into the SSMC compound.

Brash came out to meet the car. He opened Garland's door, helped her out and gave her a kiss on the cheek with a shy smile that looked completely out of place on a wickedly handsome biker. He still wasn't completely used to having a mom who doted on him and thought he was just plain wonderful head to toe.

"Brash, this is Bud," she said.

"Welcome." He gave Bud a glance and then turned his attention to his dad.

"You got news?" Brant asked. Brash nodded slightly. "Okay then." To Garland he said, "Can you show her around?"

"Of course," Garland answered.

"Oh. And I need one of you women to take her shopping. Cann said she doesn't have any clothes, but she does have some money."

Garland practically squealed. "My favorite sort of circumstance. When need and money meet, there's a good time to be had by all."

Bud smiled, but said, "I don't think I ought to spend money on…"

"Don't be silly," said Garland. "No right-headed woman turns down clothes. It's a rule."

"Well…"

"The subject is closed. We'll go shopping tomorrow after your appointment."

"I…"

"Come on. Brant said to show you around so that's what we must do. The king has spoken."

"Do you live here, too?"

Garland laughed. "No. We have a place close to downtown, overlooking the river. We'll have you over one of these days."

"That would be nice."

Garland reached over and put Bud's hair behind her shoulder. It didn't need to be done. It was an affectionate gesture that had Bud wondering what it would have been like if her mom had lived. Perhaps Garland was also wondering what it would have been like to have a daughter.

Everyone turned to look when Garland and Bud came through the door. Brant and Brash had already disappeared into Brant's office.

"Brenda, this is Bud. Your replacement. You do a good job of showing her the ropes and there'll be a nice farewell bonus in it for you."

"Yes, ma'am." Brenda smiled at Garland and at Bud. She was a sweet-looking woman in her late twenties with a round face, strawberry-blonde hair, rosy cheeks, and a full figure. But the important thing was that her welcome seemed sincere. "First thing tomorrow?"

"Sure," said Bud. "Good."

"Let me show you which room is yours," Garland said as she walked toward a long hall with doors on either side, hotel style. She stopped two doors before the end, where there were two large double doors.

Bud glanced at the number next to the door. Nine.

"This is you," Garland said as she opened the door. The room was large, made to feel even more so by the fact that there was little furniture. "Don't worry about the lack of style. You can do what you want with the place." She looked at the inside of the door, pulled a key from the deadbolt lock, and handed it to Bud. "This is the only key. If you lose it, we'll get a locksmith, but we want you to feel safe. Now sometimes the men who live here get a little rowdy. Sometimes they bring women back here. Just ignore it. They absolutely will not bother you. On pain of death."

Bud barked out a laugh at that. "Pain of death?"

Garland gave her most serious look and said, "Definitely."

"Good to know." She looked around. "This is so nice of you."

Garland shook that off. "Now about tonight. Here are your choices. You can stay in here and get settled. You can eat in the kitchen with whoever is here and start getting to know them. You could bring food back here if you want. The laundry is on the other side of the kitchen if you need it, but Brenda will give you a tour in the morning."

Bud could see that Garland was waiting for an answer. "I guess I'll, um, get settled and eat in the kitchen. No point in hiding in here. But…"

"What? Don't be afraid to say what's on your mind around here. Believe me. Everybody else does."

"Will somebody tell me what's going on with Johns? I don't know what to expect. Can he have phone calls or visitors or…? I don't know."

Garland's face softened. "Brant will let you know the second he knows anything. Now I'll be here tomorrow at eleven fifteen to pick you up for the doctor. We'll go shopping after that."

"Thank you."

"If you think you're okay, I'm going home. Is there anything else I can do for you first? You want me to introduce you to everyone?"

"They all know who I am. Right?"

"Yes. They do. They're all going to think you hung the moon because of what you said about Cann. So don't worry about being accepted. You already are. Now that you live here, think of the kitchen as yours. You can go down there any time of the day or night and get anything you want."

Bud nodded. "Thank you," she said again.

"It's not a gift. Just a statement of the way the place works." Garland patted her on the forearm. "See you tomorrow."

When she left, Bud found herself alone for the first time since Cann had told her to come out from behind the vending machines and state her business. She sat down on the bed and looked around the room. She hadn't just been saying she was grateful that she'd landed on her feet. She was grateful all the way down to her toenails. But she was also eaten alive with guilt that Cannon Johns was in jail while she was sitting in a nice safe, dry room.

She thought about crying for a few seconds, but decided it would be a waste of time. It wouldn't change a thing, wouldn't help Cann in any way, and being overly emotional might be bad for the baby.

So she got up, used the toilet and unpacked her few things from the fabulous Brahmin bag she'd essentially swiped from a rich woman who had, by all appearances, settled for money instead of love. As Bud ran her fingers over the beautiful bag she tried to imagine why someone would make that choice because, certainly, nothing in the world could be better than being loved.

Bud changed into the skinny jeans, the tunic top, and the low-heeled sandals, thinking that might be more appropriate. She opened the door and walked down the hall, but everything was quiet. There was nobody in the bar or in the lounge area, but she heard laughter coming from further back in the building.

Following the sound, she walked the length of the bar, turned left and headed into the part of the complex that was the heart of the club; the kitchen, pantry, laundry, and covered walkway to the warehouse that served as a garage for a wide array of vehicles. Behind that was the kennel and Rescue's cottage where he gave three dogs sleepover privileges every night.

When she entered the kitchen everything came to a full stop.

Bud stood one step inside the doorway taking in the scene. It was a large commercial kitchen that was a study in stainless steel. Refrigerators, sinks, cabinets, gas ranges, and ovens lined the walls. In the middle of the large room was a stainless steel island, long, narrow and counter height, that doubled as a dining table. Stools with arms and leather seats and backs were sturdy enough for big rambunctious bikers. There were enough to seat thirty people at a time.

While the stainless steel was without color, the room was not. The walls above the cabinetry were painted with murals of Austin scenes and classic motorcycles in vibrant hues that brought both life and warmth to the room. The pièce de résistance was a counter height fireplace framed in red brick that sat between ovens and gas ranges.

She fell in love with it instantly.

Eight faces congregated near the end of the island/table closest to her turned toward her expectantly. Brenda and seven bikers. She recognized a few from the night she and Cannon had arrived and there was Brash, whom she'd met that afternoon. Beautiful Brash. She was sure that, if she'd seen him first, she'd be crushing hard.

Sitting at the end near the door, he gave Bud a big grin and pushed the stool next to him with his foot. "Come on over here and sit, darlin'. We're having some of Brenda's gooey chicken enchiladas."

She gave Brash a grateful smile for being welcoming and took a seat on the stool. "Thank you."

"I'm not normally here 'cause I'm a married guy with an actual life." Some of the others scoffed. One threw a tortilla chip at his head.

"Hey!" Brenda said in a schoolteacher voice. She had gotten up to get Bud a place setting, but whirled around with hands on her hips. "How many times I gotta tell you? The food is for eating. So grow the hell up and eat."

Brash turned back to Bud with a smile. "I was sayin' that I'm not usually here, but my wife is out with girlfriends, faculty members at U.T. You're probably thinkin' that doesn't sound like a good time and I'd have to agree. But it takes all kinds to fill up the freeways. Right?"

"Right," Bud said as Brenda put a plate and flatware in front of her.

Brenda patted Bud on the shoulder. "You get whatever you want to drink out of that cooler over there." She pointed to a glass front cooler stocked with bottled waters, soft drinks, and beer.

"Thank you," she said, sliding off the stool.

As she was grabbing a water, Brash began introducing her to the other people in the room.

"Arnold. Axel. Burn. Car lot. Eric. Rescue."

"Nice to meet you," she said as she sat down, feeling a little shy about being the center of attention. "I hope I can remember your names."

"Well, let's see if we can help you with that." Brash smiled. "Arnold is easy because the resemblance is uncanny. Rescue, down there at the end, is easy because he always looks like the crazy homeless guy who won't make eye contact. Eric. Just think Eric the Viking. The fact that he's taller than a person should be will help you remember. As for the others, they're just not that important."

"Hey," came a chorus of voices and half a basket of tortilla chips was thrown at Brash's head.

Brenda turned even redder than usual and looked ready to pull the bazooka out from behind the giant sack of flour.

"I'm not pickin' those up," she said.

"Yeah." Brash glared at the others. "Pick those up."

Axel and Burn got up and picked the chips off the floor even though Bud knew for a fact they hadn't thrown them.

She leaned toward Brash and said, "They're not the ones who did it."

Brash gave her a charmingly amused smirk. "They're prospects, darlin'. It's their job to clean up after patched-in members."

"Oh." She looked down at the plate where Brenda was delivering chicken enchiladas from a casserole dish with a spatula. "This smells…"

Eric jumped in. "Taste it. It's as good as it smells. We're sure hopin' you've got some kitchen chops because Brenda here is gonna leave some big shoes to fill."

Brenda returned to her seat beaming from the compliment. "Don't you worry," she said to Bud. "These boys will eat anything. Raw. Burned. Too much tabasco. Don't matter. They're eating machines."

Bud nodded and smiled. "That's good to know."

"So tell us about your best stuff. What do we have to look forward to?" Eric asked.

"For dinner?" He nodded. "Well, I make a decent stuffed pork chop. I use my own cornbread dressing, I add pecans, sage, and onions. Top it with a brown gravy." The men exchanged looks. "I know how to fry chicken with honey in the batter. I make a pretty respectable chicken fried steak. I'm good at spaghetti and lasagna. My daddy would ask for meatloaf once a week. I like it with tomato sauce, but I can do it with brown gravy, too. I make a white cheese macaroni and cheese to go with it. My daddy says I make the best whipped potatoes in Texas. When I can get 'em, I like to do fresh black-eyed peas. We could do a fried catfish night. I have a recipe for hushpuppies that I found in an old cookbook. Hushpuppies are hard to get just right. Takes some practice."

She took another bite of chicken enchiladas and realized that everyone had stopped eating and was staring at her like she was telling tales from the *Arabian Nights*.

"Um. Did I say something I shouldn't have?"

Brenda laughed. "No. You just sent these guys into

food fantasy stupor."

Arnold cleared his throat. "That all sounds really good."

The others nodded.

Bud smiled and glanced at Brash. It only took ten minutes for the novelty that was Bud to wear off and the room was once again alive with conversation and laughter.

Bud got up to help clear dishes.

"Now you know I told you that you don't need to start till tomorrow mornin'."

"I know," Bud said, "but I'm not busy. And you can tell me how to make gooey chicken enchiladas while we're cleaning up?"

Brenda smiled. "Get an apron over there." She jerked her head toward the tall cabinets. "I can tell you're gonna work out fine, which'll make it easier for me to leave. I don't know what Brant told you about the work, but the job title should be *house mother*."

When Bud saw that Brash was leaving the room, she hurried after him and touched his shoulder. When he turned around, she said, "Any news?"

His eyes flicked back and forth between hers like he was reading her. "You know what an arraignment is?"

"Not really."

"It's when somebody accused of a crime goes in front of a judge and says whether they're guilty or not guilty."

Brash saw concern jump into the girl's facial features. "When is it?"

"Day after tomorrow."

"He's not guilty."

Brash smiled. "I know that. Matter of fact the whole world knows it. Lot of people on TV sayin' it's your pop who ought to be under arrest. Course that's not gonna happen. But he has been persuaded to tell the judge that it was all a misunderstanding and not a kidnapping, as he'd originally said."

Bud blinked twice while trying to process that. "My daddy's gonna say he didn't mean it?"

"Yep."

"That doesn't sound like him."

"Well, with a little pressure applied just right, motives can almost always be manipulated into a better attitude."

She stared at Brash. "Wow."

"Yep."

"Is this a safe place to be?"

"The safest. Why would you ask that question?"

She debated whether or not to answer directly, but concluded that Brash was the kind of man who would know if she was lying. "I know what happened to Johns' family."

Brash's face went dead serious. After a brief pause, he said, "That was tragic. First off, it's been a long time since this club was into income production of a dubious nature. And I hope this doesn't sound callous because that's not what's in my heart. But second, what you're talkin' about didn't happen here."

Bud nodded. "I'm not asking for me. I…"

"I know," he interrupted. "You've got somebody else to think about. Did you see the six o'clock news?"

"No."

"Brenda," Brash turned to where she was working over the sink, "did you record the six o'clock news?"

"Sure did. Figured there'd be somethin' about Cann on."

"I'm takin' this girl out to the bar then."

"Okay." She looked over her shoulder at Bud. "I start cookin' breakfast at seven."

"I'll be here," Bud said.

THERE WERE THREE big screen TVs in the bar and lounge area of the clubhouse that were synced by AV control. That system had nothing to do with the bank of sixteen screens showing camera angles of every inch of the building exterior, gates, and periphery of the compound.

What was currently playing on the three big screens was the first *John Wick*.

Without asking for permission, Brash claimed the remote that was velcroed to the back wall of the bar so that the bartender always had final say, and accessed the evening news as recorded a couple of hours earlier.

KXAN headline was about the arrest of Cannon Johns and the extraordinary story of rescuing a young woman and her unborn child.

Seeing Johns put in handcuffs threatened to bring tears to her eyes all over again. It was the first time she'd seen herself on TV. Her reaction was a strange mix of fascination and embarrassment, but overall, she thought she'd done a fair job of leaving the impression that Johns was not just an innocent man, but a modern day knight.

What came next were the scenes Brant had described. More crowds like the ones in Del Rio. Only bigger. As Brant had said there were two locations where people were gathering, the District Court and the capitol.

The next item was a surprise. It was her father standing in front of the Austin Ranger office being interviewed by local press. Flashes were going off so fast that it almost mimicked rapid fire weapons.

"Mr. McIntyre, have you changed your accusation that Cannon Johns kidnapped your underage daughter?"

The man looked both stony and bitter. "It was all a misunderstanding."

"But he still transported a minor across an international border without documentation of permission. That's a very serious offense."

"What the judge decides about that is out of my hands."

"Have you spoken to your daughter since you saw her at Del Rio?"

"No," he said simply, and walked away with people firing questions at him.

Brash handed the remote to Eric so that he could find his place in *John Wick* and restart his movie.

"How serious is it?" she asked Brash. "The crossing border thing."

Brash shrugged. "It'll be up to the judge, but judges

have motives that can be massaged just like everybody else."

Bud stared again. "Wow. I don't think I want to be on the wrong side of you guys."

Brash gave her a blinding smile. "You don't. And darlin', I know you don't mean anything by it, but if my wife sees you lookin' at me like that you're gonna find out why redheads have a reputation for temper." Bud gaped. "It's okay. I get it a lot. Just so you know. There's another guy who comes around here sometimes, looks a whole lot like me. Also married."

Arnold was walking by when he said that and corrected, "He doesn't look a whole lot like you. He looks *exactly* like you."

Brash shrugged. "Identical twins." While Bud tried to picture that, he went on. "Stop worryin' about Cann. It's all gonna be fine." He chuckled. "Except that he may find that celebrity doesn't sit well with him."

"Celebrity," she repeated, taking on a whole new worry she hadn't considered before. "You mean like people stopping him on the street?"

"Yeah." Brash grinned. "Like that. If it happens, it won't be a bad thing. Right now he's adored by the multitudes. He just may not like being recognized by strangers. He's been livin' under the radar for a long time."

It wasn't hard to comprehend what Brash meant. "You don't think he'll, um, run again, do you?"

Brash gave her a funny look. "Run?" He seemed to

think that over and then sighed deeply. "Honestly. I don't know. You givin' him a reason to stay?"

"If he'll let me."

"Good enough."

Bud went to bed with a whole new worry. The day had started with her worrying about whether or not Cann would do time in jail. It ended with her worrying about what Cann would do when he was released.

Bud used the alarm clock by the bed to be sure she was up and in the kitchen at seven. As it happened, she beat Brenda there by ten minutes and was trying to figure out how to use the coffee machine.

"Aren't you the early bird?" Brenda said. "Here. Like this."

She showed Bud how to use the coffee maker. "Sometimes it's persnickety. It's a six thousand dollar machine. Thinks it's a racehorse, but all we really need here is a mule. The guys don't know great coffee from spit. I don't know why Brant insists on havin' the best of everything, but he does. Nothin's too good for these big babies you've signed on to take care of. Brant lived here most of his life. Raised Brash here, too. But when Brand and Garland came to Austin, Brant got his own place."

"Brash has a twin, but they didn't grow up together?"

"Oh, darlin'. That's a story. Let's get breakfast out of the way then you and I'll sit down and visit for a bit."

Bud grinned, thinking, how bad could a job be that started off with gossip?

"Today I'm makin' the blow-it-all-the-way-out big hit breakfast that's gonna make 'em love you more than their real mamas."

Bud giggled. "Okay."

"Get yourself an apron. You know where they are. Now you don't have to do laundry for these boys unless you want the extra money. Couple of 'em'll pay you to get out of doin' for themselves." She shook her head. "Shit. They can be lazy fuckers. But you do have to launder the aprons and kitchen towels. I usually throw 'em in with my own stuff. Saves me time."

Bud nodded. "What's the blow-it-all-the-way-out big hit breakfast?"

"Christ, you got a good memory. That's gonna be a help. 'Cause the sooner you're the rubber meetin' the road, the sooner I can get outta here and be with my sweetie."

Bud smiled. "What's he like?"

Brenda stopped setting things out on the counter long enough to get a dreamy look on her face. "Handsome. Quiet." She wiggled her eyebrows at Bud. "Hung. With buns of steel." Bud couldn't help but laugh at that last part. "He's carryin' a little extra above the belt, too. He likes his beer. But nothin' wrong with that. You know?" Bud didn't know. She was eighteen and interested in flat tummies with well-defined abs, but she nodded to be polite. "He's steady. Even-tempered. In for the long haul. You know, all the things a right-headed woman wants."

Bud found herself continuing to nod without even realizing she was doing it.

"So about breakfast…" Brenda said.

"You got me off track by talking about buns and…"

"Dick."

"Um, yeah. I think we need to separate those conversations. Back to the BIATWO breakfast."

"BIATWO. I love it," Brenda said. "Look here. It's so simple it'll make you cry. You just get these breaded chicken filets out of the frozen chicken and fish section at the HEB. You bake 'em in the oven for twenty, twenty-five minutes. Now at the same time, you're poppin' Eggo waffles out of that row of toasters there." Brenda took a stack of eight plates and separated them so that they were eight individual plates sitting at the end of the island/table. She then pulled two kinds of syrup out of the refrigeration unit and set them next to the plates. "Grab eight paper napkins out of that drawer right there." She set two coffee mugs down by the plates. "Put eight forks in here and eight butter knives in here."

While Bud was doing that, Brenda went on. "Now here's the part that's gonna make you swoon. All you have to do is put those Eggo waffles on a plate, set a chicken filet on top, and let the takers squeeze out their syrup of choice. Sounds simple. Is simple. But they will think you're the greatest thing since the vagina was invented."

Bud couldn't help but laugh at the outrageous things Brenda said. Brenda was causing Bud to wonder, even if she could do the work, if she would ever develop the larger-than-life personality that Brenda wielded so effortlessly, and she wondered if that was what was required to ride herd on a bunch of bikers armed with tortilla chips.

Just as she'd said, the bikers wandered in between seven thirty and nine, grabbed a plate, poured syrup on the chicken and waffles with various expressions of approval that all meant, "Oh boy! Chicken and waffles!"

As she and Brenda cleaned up from breakfast, Brenda talked nonstop about such things as how the second dishwasher door could stick sometimes and how Brant was a stickler for cleanliness in the kitchen. Brenda wore her hair pulled back into a ponytail, then netted that into a bun. The result made her look more like the cover of Town and Country than biker club cook.

"So I suggest you find a way to keep that pretty hair of yours out of the food or you may see the ugly side of the prez."

Bud was pretty sure she didn't want to see the ugly side of the prez. "Okay. I like what you've done. Maybe I'll try that."

"Honey, it's like the chicken and waffles. Easy breezy but oh so good."

When they were finished, they poured coffee and sat down for the story Brenda had promised. Bud thought it was one of the strangest family stories she'd ever heard, but heartbreakingly romantic. She also knew for a fact that it ended well, because she'd spent hours with Brant and Garland the day before and, if there was ever a couple who belonged together, it was the two of them. Anyone could see it.

Brenda looked at her watch. "Now you don't have to worry about lunch. They're on their own and they're usually gone in the middle of the day doin' whatever it is they do. Rescue's always here, of course, because he works here. Now, once I'm gone, he'll try to talk you into cookin' for those dogs. You just tell him no. Your job is to cook for humans. Not dogs. Tell him he can cook for the dogs at his own place.

"So between breakfast and five o'clock you restock the kitchen and the bar. Do what cleanin' needs to be done. Got a service that comes twice a week to do such things as sweepin', dustin', vacuumin', and cleanin' the bathrooms. Oh. Trust me, girl. You would *not* want to be them!" She was shaking her head and making a face. "Also, if somebody left a whore layin' around with no clothes on their nasty skanky asses, let the cleanin' people find 'em and not you."

Bud looked curious. "Does that really happen or are you makin' it up?"

Brenda took in a long indulgent breath. "The boys are red-blooded and some of 'em don't know that all pussy's not the same. Brant discourages that behavior these days, but he doesn't say no. They're grown ass men." She shrugged. "Just how it is. They won't bother you though. Brant read them the Riot Act and Brash is Enforcer. Nobody wants to be enforced by Brash. Believe me. So no matter how cute they may think you are, they're gonna leave you the hell alone.

"Now when it comes to meal plannin', you're in charge. In your condition, you got special needs. And you need to put yourself first when you're thinkin' about what to serve. If that means the men have to eat salads with grilled chicken instead of fried chicken, then so be it. It wouldn't hurt them to be a little health conscious."

Bud grinned. "I think they'd hate me."

"Now you listen to me and hear me well. Two weeks from now you're not going to care what they think about you. They're the ones who need to be turnin' themselves inside out worried about whether or not *you're* feeling all right. The woman who controls the food and the drink is all powerful. Never forget that. Men can do without anything else. Anything. But they've got to have their food and drink."

For a full minute Bud sat and processed that. Then she laughed out loud. "You're sayin' that, when it comes to the Sons of Sanctuary clubhouse, I'm all powerful."

"Hmmm. I wouldn't cross Brant if I were you. Other than that, yes. You're the shit." Without missing a beat, Brenda continued, "So the cleanin' you need to do is mostly in here." She looked around the kitchen. "And the bar. I'll show you the ins and outs of how all that works.

"Now the guys will start driftin' in wantin' alcoholic beverages around five. You warm up the TVs and give them a first round. You don't need to learn about mixed drinks. The bar motto is keep it simple. When you need to start dinner, one of them can hand out beers and pour whiskey. After all, there's only one of you. Right?"

There was only one answer to that. "Right."

"So the job hours are kind of different. You'll be in here cookin' breakfast at seven and I'm usually out there at the bar until ten. I leave the bar sparklin' before I go to bed. If somebody makes a mess after that, they're not gonna like me in the mornin'. You know what I mean?" Bud nodded. "Good news is that there's a lot of time between breakfast and five for you to run your own errands and, most importantly, get a nap. As your pregnancy progresses, you're probably gonna need that more and more."

Brenda was showing Bud around the bar when Garland swept in.

"Good morning." She smiled at Bud and Brenda.

"Hey, boss lady," Brenda said.

Garland scowled at Bud. "Please do not call me that. Ever." She looked at Brenda. "She does it just to aggravate me." Brenda laughed. "You ready?" she asked Bud. "That's a beautiful top you're wearing."

"Thank you." Bud had to agree. She wasn't sorry she'd snagged the rose tunic even if it had been a favorite of Señora Gutierrez.

GARLAND AND BUD were twenty minutes early for her appointment. The doctor was running forty minutes late.

"It's very nice of you to do this," Bud told Garland.

"Have you been to see an obstetrician before?" Garland asked. Bud shook her head. "Gynecologist?"

Bud shook her head again.

Garland contemplated whether or not she should say something about pelvic exams, but decided maybe it would be best not to have Bud form preconceived ideas based on someone else's experience. She'd taken care to get Bud a woman OBGYN. Not only would it seem less humiliating to someone with Bud's age and inexperience, but the doctor's hands, like the rest of her, were smaller.

Garland tried to ignore the TV monitor so that she could read her book while Bud was with the doctor, and part of her longed for the days when there was peace to be found in public places.

Bud came out clutching a white paper bag. Garland rose and met her at checkout.

"Samples of vitamins," Bud said, raising the bag.

"Good. I know you need those."

Garland paid the bill. On the way out she said, "Now for the fun part. Are you hungry?"

"Unbelievably, yes. Even though I had chicken and waffles for breakfast."

"I'm sure you just got a lecture about diet."

"Yeah."

"Well, you can get serious about that right after I take you to Torchy's Tacos."

Torchy's was a permanent food truck on a gravel parking lot, but there was a building next to it that was basically a screened-in porch with picnic tables inside. Garland was right about the food. Bud had shrimp tacos with caramelized onions.

"So what kinds of things are we shopping for?"

"I pretty much left everything at home when I ran. I need tennis shoes and underwear and, I guess, lots of jeans and tops. Judgin' from my morning with Brenda, seems like the tennis shoes are going to be the most important thing. I have some pesos to exchange…"

"Give me those," Garland said.

Bud fished the pesos out of her purse and handed them over without question. Garland took out her phone and looked up the exchange rate. "That's $7.65." Garland pulled a ten out of her purse and put it on the table. "I'll take the $2.35 out of your first paycheck."

That was the first time Bud had thought about a paycheck. She'd been so stunned with the roller coaster ride she'd been on the day before, and they'd been so generous, she hadn't thought to ask.

"We didn't discuss pay with you, did we?" Bud shook her head. "Well, it's a thousand dollars a week."

"How much is my room and food and health insurance?"

"Oh no. It's a thousand dollars *after* those things. And you do get paid for training. So you're actually earning money for today."

Bud was stunned. That meant that she was going to be able to save most of her pay. She couldn't have been more surprised, or elated, if she'd been told she'd won the lottery.

"That's… kind of amazing. Am I on…um."

"Probation?"

"Yes."

"No. Because you came with a strong reference from a club member."

"Oh."

"And I can tell, after knowing you for twenty-four hours, that you're the kind of person who takes obligations seriously. Somewhat unusual for someone your age."

"I have five hundred dollars left, but three of it really belongs to Johns. He handed it to me before they," she looked down, "um, took him."

"Cann doesn't intend for you to give that money back. He gave it to you so you would have it for yourself. For reasons just such as this."

"How do you know that?"

"Woman's intuition. But never mind. If it makes you feel better, I'll give you an advance on your first payday."

"That would be great."

"Good. It's decided. Now where shall we go?"

"I don't really know Austin."

"Pshhhh. These days every place is the same. I don't know about you, but I hate malls. How about if we go to the shoe warehouse first? We can get your jeans, tops, and undies at a single department store. If you need toiletries, we can do that at a drug store or Target. How does that sound?"

"Perfect. But I think I need to be back in time to help with dinner."

Garland smiled. "Today's not a full work day. It's about doctors and shopping."

"I need hairnets. I've never used them, but I think it looks better than a baseball hat. You know, the way Brenda wears her hair."

"Good call. It's very attractive."

By the time Garland pulled into the SSMC it was dinner time. She'd already alerted Brant that she was eating there tonight. So he'd told Brenda to plan on two extra. He knew that Brenda went to some extra fuss when she knew Garland was coming. She loved the lavish attention and praise. Garland was masterful at making people feel good about themselves.

While they'd been at Target, Garland guided her to the bedding department and gave her a five hundred dollar allowance for personalizing her room at the clubhouse. When Bud had finally balked at the generosity, Garland insisted.

Consequently there was a lot of stuff in the car including new pillows, comforter, sheets, towels, and a flower vase covered with brightly colored, mirrored mosaic squares.

Garland told Axel to help Bud with the bags.

"Yes, ma'am," he said dutifully without a trace of sarcasm. Brant was a tyrant about knowing whom to respect along with when and how to give it. It took two trips for him to deliver everything.

Bud had never been on what might be called a shopping 'spree' in her life. It had been fun to get a bunch of new things and it had been fun to do it with a woman who helped make decisions. There had been times during the afternoon when she'd gone for as long as ten minutes without thinking about Johns.

She pulled out new jeans that were less chic, more her style, pulled on a plain knit top, and practically groaned from the pleasure of comfort when she put on one of the two pairs of thick-soled sneakers she'd bought.

There were a few more people for dinner than the night before. She took an apron out of the cupboard and was putting it on when she arrived at the sink.

"How can I help?" she asked Brenda.

"Did you get what you need?"

"Yeah. Thanks."

Brenda nodded toward vegetables set out on the big cutting board. "Finish chopping those up, toss that salad, and get all the different kinds of salad dressing out of that refrigerator over there."

"Okay."

Bud sliced tomatoes, boiled eggs, green peppers, red onion, and cucumbers. Threw them into two giant wooden bowls with the hearts of romaine. Tossed. Then pulled about seven different varieties of salad dressing bottles out of the unit that seemed to contain mostly cooking ingredients that required refrigeration.

"Done," she said to Brenda.

"Okay. Start sending those bowls of salad around."

Bud took the first bowl to Garland and said, "Salad, madam?"

Garland chortled. "Much better than that thing Brenda calls me." She took the salad and Bud went back for more.

When everyone was seated and eating, Bud filled a plate with chicken breasts coated in cornflakes, au gratin potatoes, tossed salad, and soft flakey crescent rolls fresh from the oven. She sat at the furthest end of the table, happy to just listen and be out of the hurricane's eye of attention.

Somebody named Crow told a story about a guy walking by the side of the road smoking a cigarette, wearing nothing but combat boots and tighty whities. Everybody accused him of making it up, but he swore it was true.

After cleanup, Bud accompanied Brenda to the bar where her education continued. "And you don't have to put up with porn on the big screens if you don't want to. Just tell the lunkheads to take their pervy little selves to their own rooms. Every one of them has a TV. They can watch other people pretend to get off in their own rooms."

Bud smiled, but secretly hoped she would never have to ask any of those men to, um, take their hobbies elsewhere.

THE NEXT DAY was nonstop apprenticing, but Bud was a fast learner and she was beginning to feel like she had a handle on things already.

"Now if you get under the weather, don't worry. Everybody gets sick sometimes and we have ways of dealin' with it. You let Arnold know first. He's in number three. He'll take care of the rest startin' with breakfast. The man actually knows how to make bacon and eggs.

"If you need to go to the doctor, he'll take you. If you need cold stuff from the pharmacy, he'll get it for you. If you just need to stay in bed and slurp hot chicken soup, he'll manage that, too."

"That's good."

"So neither of us got a nap today, but you learned so much I think you could take over if you needed to."

Bud paled visibly as she looked at Brenda, shaking her head no. "Uh, no. No. I'm not… not ready."

"What are you afraid of?"

Bud looked toward the guys sitting at the bar talking and watching TV, then looked back at Brenda. "Them."

"Well," Brenda smiled, "the only way you'll get past that is for me to get out of the way so you can find your own way and forge your own relationships with the crew."

Bud had a feeling there was no point in arguing. "Are you leaving, like, now?"

Brenda laughed. "No. Not until next week sometime. Stop lookin' like a rabbit. Where's that girl that stood up and told her daddy, the Ranger, to take a hike?"

"I don't know."

"No. That's not the answer. The answer is, right here." She patted her own chest. "Come on. Say it."

"Right here?" Bud said.

Brenda cocked one hip and put her hand on it. "I'm not convinced."

"Right here," Bud said a little forcefully.

"Better. We'll work on it."

Brash stopped by a few minutes after five and asked Bud for a Lone Star. When she set it in front of him, he said, "You want to go to the arraignment tomorrow? Things…"

"Yes." She didn't let him finish before she answered definitely.

Brash smirked good-naturedly. "I was gonna say that if things go our way, he'll be comin' back here with us. Things don't go our way, you'll at least get to see him. Know he's okay."

She looked at Brash with big clear eyes. "What time?"

"Pick you up at nine."

"Thank you."

"No reason. You know, Cann and I were prospects together. We're the same age. It made us, I don't know, I guess you'd say close. Guys who prospect together, it's a bond you don't have with other…" He stopped and looked around, almost like he'd be embarrassed to be overheard talking about feelings. "I'm glad he's back. Hope he's gonna stay. There's a place here for him."

Bud nodded. "What was he like? Before?"

Brash grinned. "He knew how to have fun, but he was never one to drink too hard or whore around. He saw a future with the club and took it seriously. He was a good storyteller. And he can sing."

"He told me he couldn't."

"He told you he couldn't sing?"

"Yes. He brought me a birthday cupcake with a candle and said, 'Please don't ask me to sing, 'cause I can't'."

Brash looked serious all of a sudden. "Well, I guess he had his reasons."

"Something to do with her."

Brash stared at Bud for a few seconds before saying, "Probably."

"It's all right. I'm not going to be able to tiptoe around it. It's going to come up and it won't break me when it does."

Brash nodded with a deep sigh, knocked on the bar, and said, "Nine," as he turned to go.

Bud put on her tan dress to go to court and sat watching the monitor that displayed the camera feed trained on the gate. She didn't know what Brash's car looked like, but she figured anybody coming in at that time was probably him.

When a black SUV pulled up, the gate opened.

"Time to go," Arnold said loud enough for everybody in the building to hear him.

Bud watched as ten bikers pulled in behind the SUV. She was right behind Arnold as he left the clubhouse and she was followed out by everybody but Brenda, Axel and Burn.

She walked toward the SUV with the back door standing open. A redhead was driving. Garland was in the passenger seat and another younger blonde was in the back.

Brash came up and took her by the elbow. "You ride with my mom and my wife. Okay?" He pulled her to a stop. "Oh. And this is my brother, Brandon."

Bud turned and realized why Brash had warned her about his twin. It was kind of a shock to see such striking guys 'looking better than a body has a right to'.

"Hi," she said.

Brand nodded.

Brash opened the back door to the SUV. "That's my wife, Brigid, driving. This is Brand's wife, Cami. We're a close bunch. What happens to Cann happens to everybody."

Bud tried to process that, but given her experience, that sense of community was unfathomable. She'd pretty much lived her life as a family of one; herself. On the occasion when her dad was in the same place at the same time, he wasn't especially interested in what might be going on with her.

She got in the backseat with Cami. As Brash closed the door, Garland turned around. "Like he said, these are my daughters-in-law. I did okay for myself on that score." She smiled. "I can see you're nervous and that's understandable. But I think those Christians are ready to tear the courthouse down if the judge doesn't free their hero."

"Everybody knows there's nobody more bloodthirsty than Christians," said the redhead behind the wheel.

Garland rolled her eyes. "Brigid is an intellectual. I

don't know if I agree with her assessment..."

"Ask the millions who died in the Crusades," Brigid interjected.

"But," Garland continued, "in this case, I do hope they insist on having their way."

"Hear. Hear," said Cami. When Bud looked over at her, she smiled. "Don't worry. He'll be having dinner here tonight."

Bud wished she had that kind of confidence. She stretched her neck to see the time on the dashboard. "What time is the, um, thing?"

"Arraignment," Brigid said. "Ten."

Bud took in a deep breath, just before a roar began that sounded loud enough to open the earth. She looked around. The engines of twenty-three motorcycles had come to life at once. Half of those, including Brant, Brash, and Brand roared past them, out of the gate and onto the gravel road that would take them to the state road that would take them to Austin.

Brigid pulled in behind Eric and Car Lot. The other bikers came up behind them. When they reached the state road, there were easily another fifty bikers who fell in behind the columns.

"Who are they?" asked Bud.

"Mostly hobbyists who are friends of the club, but there are also members from two other clubs who are riding along as a show of respect for the SSMC and for Cann."

Bud was overwhelmed by the show of support. It

wasn't just strangers anymore. It was people who cared about him. As she rode along, barely seeing the scrub brush through the side window, she remembered their exchange in the solarium.

No more than three nights.

That's how long it had been. Three nights in jail. She hoped there was a god of wishes who took such pronouncements seriously.

THEY WERE LATE getting into the court room because of the crowds and because the court room was already full. Brandon had to pull some last minute strings to get Bud in, but he took her by the elbow and ushered her in, holding the door.

When Cann turned around, her eyes locked on his immediately. Until she was there, she'd been halfway expecting chains and an orange jumpsuit. But he was in his own clothes, although not the same ones he'd been wearing when he was arrested. No chains. No handcuffs.

She smiled and held up three fingers.

He nodded. He understood.

And ten minutes later, he was free to go with a sentence of twenty hours of community service. He was not to leave the county until that service had been completed.

He shook hands with the lawyer provided by the club.

When he tried to leave, he was mobbed by people who wanted to shake his hand or get an interview on camera or just say how much they thought of him. It took half an hour to get to where the club had his bike waiting.

They all congratulated him.

He looked around for Bud. Brash told him that she was riding in the SUV. He looked her direction, but couldn't see inside with the dark tinted glass. He nodded to Brash, pulled on his cut, and got on his bike. He rode beside Brash on the way back to the SSMC.

It couldn't be said that he felt lighthearted. He might never feel lighthearted again, but he did feel worry free. And that was something.

The party that had been planned seemed over the top for the occasion, but bikers would use any excuse as a good reason to party. By the time the women had parked and walked inside, Cann was surrounded by bikers, many of whom had known him before he went nomad and hadn't seen or spoken to him in years. They wanted a chance to celebrate his freedom *and* his homecoming.

Bud was experiencing a classic conflict of emotion. She was thrilled, elated, that he was free. She was also dejected because she couldn't get close enough to say, "Hi. I'm glad you're free."

She knew he belonged to all those people, more than he belonged to her, and she didn't want to resent it. She also knew she should be behind the bar helping Brenda, but she couldn't make herself put on a smile. Too much emotion for one day.

So she quietly withdrew and went to her room.

She sat on the side of the bed telling herself that she was not going to cry like a baby because she was disappointed. She was a big girl, about to be somebody's mother and that was the way she'd behave.

After half an hour or so, she was thinking about taking a shower and going to bed when the door to her room opened. Her first thought was that she must have been too distracted to lock it. Her second thought was that she was glad she hadn't, because the person stepping into her room was Cannon Johns.

He looked around, took in the English floral print on the comforter, the bright mosaic flower vase that Garland had filled with gladiolas, and the myriad sizes and shapes of pillows on the bed. Women and their pillows.

"What in the world happened in here?" he said.

She stood up, hesitated for a second, then after running a few steps launched herself into the air. He caught her as she wrapped her legs around his waist. Before he could protest she was kissing him like her life depended on it. His mouth responded to her like it had a mind of its own, before he had a chance to think through what was happening and make a rational choice.

By the time his brain engaged, it just felt too good to stop.

He'd hooked up with women over the years. There was always release. There was never satisfaction. And nothing that felt like the woman currently attached to him like a monkey.

At length he pulled back and caught his breath.

"Three nights. Just like you said."

He set her down on her feet. "Don't go gettin' ideas. That didn't mean anything."

She blinked. "You mean that kiss? Of course it meant something." He shook his head. "Liar."

When he spoke, he looked sad but serious. "Not lyin'. I'm not your savior. I'm just some guy you met in a storm."

"You better check in with your heart, Johns. Mine says that's not true."

Cann saw a flash of Molly walking away into sunlight so bright he couldn't see her anymore, leaving behind a field of full blossom bluebonnets swaying in a gentle breeze.

He hesitated with his hand on the doorknob, but opened it and walked out without looking back. He walked straight past the bar and down the hall to Brant's office. He knew Brant would be there. The prez wasn't much of a party guy. He'd hang around because he didn't want to snub a celebration, but he usually handled it by making brief appearances between long periods of keeping his own company.

Cann knocked on the door and heard Brant say, "Yeah. Come on in."

Brant looked a little surprised to see him, but said, "Close the door and take a chair." Cann did exactly that. "Lot to take in for somebody who's been livin' the solitary life."

Cann nodded.

Brant pulled the good bottle of Scotch out of the file cabinet next to his desk and held it up. When Cann nodded again, Brant poured an inch in each of two glasses.

"What's on your mind?" Brant said at length.

"Bud," was all Cann said.

"What's the problem?"

"She's a kid."

"That really the problem?"

"What do you mean? I said it was."

"Don't get testy with me just because you've got your own head up your ass."

"What the fuck is that supposed to mean?"

Brant slammed the Scotch back. "I don't claim to have all the answers, but I believe that girl was put in your path at the exact moment she needed you. And I think maybe it had somethin' to do with you needin' her, too. It's always a mistake to walk away from a gift, especially when it's like a bird nest on the ground."

Cann slammed his Scotch back. "Bird nest on the ground. Where'd you hear that one?"

"I don't know. Someplace."

"I got a room?"

"Number ten. It's always been yours."

"All right."

The room filled with noise from the common rooms as soon as the door opened. Music was blasting and the guys were starting to get smashed. Brant sighed when the door closed and shut it out again. Sometimes he felt like he had to be a father to his club. Sometimes a shrink. Sometimes a priest. Sometimes he cursed his grandfather for putting him in that position. Not often though.

Cann made his way around the edges of the party without anybody noticing. When he got to number ten, he looked to his right. Bud was right across the hall. She was absolutely right. He was a liar. What he wanted more than anything was to walk right through that door, curl up in that silly flower-covered bed, and make love to her until he could remember what it felt like to be human. But that wouldn't be fair because he had a date with death.

He'd made up his mind.

He was just going to stay alive long enough to make sure that she was going to be okay. Then he was going to do it.

When Cann arrived at breakfast, Bud was buzzing around like she'd been in charge of the kitchen for years. Car Lot said something Cann couldn't hear and she laughed in response. Then she glanced up and saw him. The laughter went away fast and she turned back to the hash browns she was turning on the griddle.

"Cannon Johns," said a female voice to his left. "I'm Brenda. I've been holdin' down the fort here for a while. This girl's got the job down though. Didn't take her no time at all."

Cann nodded. "Mornin'. Smells good in here."

"Have a seat. We're doin' short order cookin' this morning. Don't do it often, but since there's two of us... How'd you like your eggs?"

"Over easy?"

Brenda eyed him up and down. "Three? Four?"

He chuckled. "Three. Please."

"He likes bacon," Bud tossed over her shoulder without looking at him.

"Okay. We got lots," Brenda said.

Cann took a seat at the table.

"You ready to go to work?" Brash asked.

"You got somethin' for me?" Cann replied, taking a sip of the coffee Brenda set in front of him.

"Always," Brash said.

"What are you doin' here anyway? Didn't I hear you got married?"

"Yeah. I'm as whipped as a man can be, but I come in for breakfast most mornings. It's easier to coordinate the day if we all start out on the same page."

That made sense to Cann. "So you're a business man. The real deal."

"It's a livin', brother."

"Speakin' of brothers. I met yours in New Mexico. It was a trip. Somebody who looks just like you, but ain't you." He shook his head. "I couldn't stop starin'."

"Damn irritatin'."

Cann laughed. "I bet."

They chatted amiably for a few minutes about the club's network of investments and small businesses.

Cann stopped when Bud set a plate down in front of him. She'd changed her shampoo, but he could still smell her underneath.

"Thank you," he said, but she didn't respond.

Brash noticed, but looked away.

THAT SET THE tone for life at the SSMC.

BRENDA LEFT FOR Arizona the next week, but by that time Bud had the confidence she needed to be the new house mom. The club members learned to love her, even more so when the pregnancy began to show.

Cann came into the kitchen one day when Axel was asking, "When are you due?"

"End of May," she'd said without turning away from the stovetop where she was working.

"Well, what are we gonna do then?" Axel almost whined.

Bud laughed. "I'm sure we'll figure it out." When she turned to look at Axel, she noticed Cann and her smile fell. As it always did.

She seemed to be doing okay, but he'd made up his mind to hold off on his plans until he knew for sure that she was going to be fine.

The weeks came and went. Her body began to swell and just before Thanksgiving, the inevitable happened. Cann arrived at the club house at four forty five, earlier than usual. Bud was already on duty behind the bar and couldn't avoid him.

"What'll you have?" she said.

"Beer. The good stuff."

"Every one of you has a different idea of what 'good stuff' means."

"The Bad Deadpool."

"Bad Deadpool it is."

She popped the top and set the ice cold bottle in front of him.

"How are you doin'?" he said.

"Okay. You?"

"Same. You like your job here?"

"Sure. Gettin' this job was like findin' a bird nest on the ground."

Cann remembered his conversation with Brant. *So that's where he heard it.*

"You feelin' good?"

"Yes."

"You need anything?"

"Look." She finally looked him in the eye. "What is this? Am I good. Do I need anything. That's horseshit. You know what I need. Either give it to me or shut up and leave me alone."

The door opened and four bikers came through, laughing about something Burn had said.

Cann swiveled on his stool, greeted them, and that was the last time he talked to Bud for a while. But he watched. Closely, from a distance.

Bud planned a huge Thanksgiving feast for the people who didn't have family. That included her. But when Thanksgiving came she was sorry she'd taken on so much. By late morning, she'd slid down the cabinets to the floor and was, more or less, wallowing in a tearful puddle.

The heavenly smell of turkey baking had wafted down the hall and caused Cann to think he had to have a snack. When he walked into the kitchen, he was instantly alarmed.

"What's wrong? Is it the baby? Do you need to go to the hospital?"

In an instant he was crouched beside her, trying to help her up.

She slapped at him. "No. It's not the baby. No. I don't need to go to the hospital. Get your big paws off of me."

"Then what's wrong?"

"It's too much. I don't think I can get it all done by myself."

The lines disappeared from Cann's forehead as his expression cleared and then softened. "Come on." He pulled her up, even though she put up some resistance, and sat her on the stool at the end of the island. "Tell me what needs to be done. You know I'm a better cook than you."

"Who says?" she sniffled.

He handed her a paper napkin to use as a tissue. "Me."

"All that corn bread and bread pieces need to be mixed together in that tub with the onions and celery. You mash it all up together and add…"

"Water. I know how to make cornbread dressing, sugar."

He could have bit through his own tongue as soon as he said it, but it was out. There it was. Whether he called her 'sugar' or not, that's how he thought of her. And now she knew it for sure.

He set a glass of sparkling cider down in front of her and told her about how satisfying it was to see what had become of the parts matchmaking business he'd started right out of high school. Brash had hired the right people to take it to a level he'd never imagined.

"That must make you feel really good," she said.

"Yeah."

"So is that what you do? When you leave here every day?"

"Things have left me behind. Brash has me working on trying to catch up, but I'm not quite there yet." He turned and smiled at her. "Not a fast learner like you."

"I'm not a fast learner. I already knew how to do the stuff I do here. I never thanked you for getting me this job. It's been so much more than I could have dreamed about. So thank you."

"You're welcome. But the only thanks I need is knowin' that you're gettin' what you need from life."

"I think we can turn the fire off under those potatoes. The dressing's going into those two turkey roasters. The last oven's big enough for them if you don't put the top on."

"Okay."

"The green beans…"

"Are in the steamer. They can wait until we're almost ready to eat."

"The standing rib…"

"Is ready. But I've got to tell you that's where you crossed the line into the ridiculous. This was too much for one person. I mean maybe if one person was doin' this for four. But look at this place. You have to cover four times as much ground as most people makin' Thanksgivin' today."

"Well, I see that now. Thank you for helping."

Between the two of them, they got Thanksgiving on the table.

After people had eaten so much they could barely move, Cann instructed Burn and Axel that Bud had the rest of the day off, that they would be cleaning up and that they'd better do it right. Then he added that they'd be expected to make turkey sandwiches later if anybody got hungry.

"Yes, sir," they said dutifully. Truthfully, they didn't mind that much. They'd both come from the kinds of families that didn't do Thanksgiving and they were grateful for the closest thing they'd ever had to a family holiday.

Cann made Bud sit down on the sofa and proclaimed that they were all going to watch whatever movie she picked out. Partly out of wickedness and partly out of desire, she chose *Beauty and the Beast*.

Cann narrowed his eyes at Bud. "Seriously?"

"Yes."

"I thought you aren't a little kid."

"I'm not a little kid, idiot. It's a story for the ages."

"For the ages," he said drily. "Jesus."

When Burn and Axel heard what was going on in the common rooms, they congratulated each other on kitchen duty.

So the bikers spent a lazy Thanksgiving afternoon watching a story about a young girl and a creature both cursed and morose. In spite of themselves, they were swept away by the story and ceased complaining until the end, when each attempted to save his reputation by renewing his objection.

"My turn," Cann said.

To everyone's surprise, he didn't choose *The Wild Bunch*, or *Armageddon*, or even a zombie movie. He chose *It's A Wonderful Life*.

Sometime after she'd fallen asleep on the sofa, Cann picked her up, carried her to bed, took off her shoes, and tucked her in. She didn't see him again for three weeks and it didn't take a genius to figure out that he was avoiding her.

She didn't know where he was staying or what he was doing and had too much pride to ask around.

CHAPTER TWELVE

ONE NIGHT SHE was still at the bar around nine when Cann came through the door. He hesitated when his eyes met hers, but he looked away quickly. There were a lot of bikes parked outside, but things were quiet and deserted in the clubhouse. He knew something was off because Rescue was on the gate. Rescue was never on the gate.

Cann headed back toward Brant's office. When he got close enough to see that nobody was there, he noticed the door to the conference room, "church" as some called it, was open. He stepped to the door and looked around the room. Though everybody except Rescue was there, it was quiet as a tomb, and every man to the last was looking grim.

"What's going on?" he said.

"Come on in," Brant said, motioning toward the empty chair and looking like he'd rather chew razor blades than be where he was.

Eric got up and closed the door before retaking his seat.

"There's no easy way to say this, brother. We found

the guy."

There was only one thing that could mean. Cann's heart almost stopped, but his mind was whirling so fast with images of the explosion, he couldn't think clearly. "The... guy? You mean...?"

Brant nodded. "Wasn't another club, which is probably why it's been a mystery for so long. We were lookin' in the wrong place." Brant paused and took in a deep breath looking like he felt absolute empathy with Cann. "This is gonna be hard to hear. Joe Reynosa."

Cann's mouth fell open in disbelief and his head began to shake back and forth. "Can't be."

Joe Reynosa had been a prospect the same time he and Brash had been workin' butts down to their assholes to get patches. In Cann's mind, Joe was a good guy who'd just busted out. Didn't have what it took. So the club had cut him loose. That was how it worked. That was how it had always worked.

"AXEL AND BURN were over at Peyote Chill earlier."

That was a bar on the far north end of Austin frequented by another club. It was the kind of club that openly pretended friendliness while hiding a shadowy agenda. One of the duties of prospects was to stop in occasionally, without colors. Just be guys getting a beer. The Peyote Chill was not the sort of place where professionals stopped for a wind down drink on the way home from work. It was rough from the front parking lot to the rear trash bins and the bathrooms needed a peroxide-

Lysol mixture sprayed through a firehose at ceilings, walls, fixtures, and floors.

"He was there, drunk and talkin'. Axel and Burn didn't know who he was and vice versa, but they do know your story." Cann's gaze flicked to Axel then Burn and back to Brant. "Joe was sayin' stuff that wouldn't make sense to anybody who didn't know the history. The short of it is that he left carryin' a grudge because he busted out and you didn't. Guess that over time it festered.

"Apparently he never intended to hurt Molly and the baby. That part was an accident. He was out for you, but it went bad." Brant paused for a second. "I guess he would have done the same thing to Brash, but Brash was livin' here and it wouldn't have been easy to get past security.

"So Axel and Burn paid up, went outside, and called Arnold to bring the van. Joe'd been drinkin' since early afternoon so he was past done by dinner time. Our boys knew it wouldn't be long before they threw him out. So they waited. Hog tied him. Put him in the back of the van. Followed Arnold back here."

After a long time, Cann said, "Jesus," so quietly it was barely audible.

"Now the next part of this is up to you. Don't have to tell you that we're committed to be law-abidin' citizens for the most part. But one of the advantages of bein' a club is that we know when that just doesn't fill the bill. Only you can tell us if this is one of those times."

"You're sayin' I've got options." Cann spoke slowly

and deliberately. The blood was throbbing in his head so hard it sounded like his voice was outside his body and muted.

"Exactly so," said Brant. "Already took a vote before you got here. And it was unanimous. Whatever you decide. That's what we're gonna do. We're all in it with you."

Cann stared at Brant for a long time. The other club members waited patiently, not making a sound. No doubt each was silently wondering what he would do if he was in the shoes of the man making the decision.

With abruptness that was startling, Cann said, "I need to talk to Bud."

As he started to get out of his chair, Brant said, "Hold on. This is club business. You know there's a tradition…"

"Don't give a damn about traditions that everybody knows are…"

"Outdated?" supplied Rally.

Cann's head jerked toward Rally. "Yes. Exactly. I'm talkin' to Bud before I decide."

"Does that even make sense, Cann? I mean wives I can see. Maybe. But Bud… Not sayin' she's not gonna grow up to be somethin' really special. That's just a ways off."

"You're wrong," said Cann. "And she's the one I'm gonna talk to."

"Cann. She comes from a law family."

"So do you!" Cann practically shouted. He was talking about the Fornight familial ties to the Rangers.

Brant let the insubordination go. It was understandable given the heat of the moment. Finally he asked, "Why?"

That question buried Cann in emotional conflict as sure as if it was weighed down by nine yards from a dump truck. He started to say, "I don't know," but stopped himself because he knew that would be dishonest. "Because she cares more about me than anybody." He looked around the room. "Even you."

Brant ran a hand through his hair, beautifully graying at his temples, and looked around the room. One by one the members gave wordless assent.

"Do it," Brant said. "We'll wait."

Bud had left the bar and gone to her room for the night. The knock on the door was a surprise. People rarely disturbed her privacy and never at that time of night. She'd taken a quick shower, tied her hair up, and put on a flannel night shirt that came to her knees. She slipped on the jackalope house shoes she'd bought on Congress Avenue and shuffled for the door.

Seeing Cann standing on the other side was fantasy combined with incongruence. She waited for him to speak.

"I need to talk to you," he said.

His face gave away that he'd just experienced some kind of upheaval and she wanted to know what it was. Stepping back, she opened the door wider as an invitation to come in. After closing it behind Cann, she walked to her bed, and sat down on the side of it.

Cann followed and sat beside her.

When he didn't begin talking, she decided to try to help. "What happened?"

As his face turned toward hers, she briefly saw torture in his eyes. Then it was gone.

"We know who did it. And why. And we have him in, ah, private custody."

It took a second for her to make the connection. Then she said, "Oh."

"I have to decide what to do."

"What do you mean?"

"With him. What to do with him."

She cocked her head, her own mind racing. "What are the options?"

"There are two. Go to jail. Disappear."

She looked away, picked a spot on the tile floor in front of her feet and stared until she nodded that she understood. "Why are you telling me?"

He barked out a laugh that held no humor. "Brant said the same thing. Not sure I can explain it really. Best I can do is say that I think you care about me. Maybe more than anybody."

He looked over at her and knew the answer to that question didn't need to be spoken.

"Do you want me to tell you what to do?" she asked quietly.

After a few beats he said, "No. I want you to tell me what you think."

She put her hand in Cann's where it was resting on

his thigh. He didn't pull away as she feared he might. "I like these people. This club has been good to me. If I understand things, it wasn't always respectable, but it is now. I wouldn't want to see anything hurt what they have here." She rushed to add, "And I'm not just sayin' that because it's good for me and the baby. But look, Johns, I want you to do the thing that will free you from the burden you're carryin'. The guilt."

Even in the dim lamplight she could see that his eyes were red around the rims. "I don't think that's goin' away. I'm good with cars. But I got so busy with the parts service, I didn't pay close enough attention to Molly's car." A big tear rolled down Cann's face and broke Bud's heart even more. "Her car didn't start because I hadn't maintained it well enough. It was my responsibility to see that she had a car runnin'. I'm the one who ought to be dust. And my little girl ought to be in first grade."

He pulled his hand away and wiped at his eyes like the tears were humiliating.

"I've heard that everybody looks for ways to blame themselves when somebody they love dies. It's natural."

"They didn't die. They were murdered. Because of me."

Bud took in a deep breath. "I know. Here's the thing. If I was Molly, I'd be wantin' you to live. Just like you wish it'd been you 'cause you'd want her to live. I think she thinks the same about you."

Cann said nothing.

"Let me ask you a question. Would you rather die or

go to jail for the rest of your life?"

He turned his face toward Bud and studied her for a couple of seconds. "Die."

She nodded. "So what's the bigger punishment?"

He nodded as he stood up and walked to the door, but when he reached it, without looking back he said, "Will you wait up for me?"

"Of course," she said. "I'll always wait for you, Johns."

CANN DELIVERED HIS verdict to the club. They called Russell, who took Joe Reynosa into custody and turned him over to the Travis County Sheriff a little the worse for wear. Cann didn't kill him, but while the other club members looked on, he had taken advantage of his chance to deliver some atavistic justice that stopped just short of killing the man.

It was after midnight when Bud heard the second knock on her door.

That time she was waiting for it.

She hurried to answer, but as soon as she opened the door, Cann pulled her up his body into a kiss that welded both souls together as the fire that had been simmering on low for so long burst into greedy, demanding flames.

He knew he'd never be free of the guilt he felt about Molly and the baby, but he also knew that they were in a place with impossibly blue skies, impossibly bright sun, light pleasant breezes, and full blown bluebonnets. She would want him to live. And maybe take care of a lost mother with a fatherless child.

As he'd wanted to do for so long.

He made love being careful of the baby bump even though Bud turned out to be cat scratch hot in bed. Her wanton leanings, while welcome, made taking care a challenge. She turned him on so fast he was afraid he might come in his pants like a fourteen-year-old.

Her breasts were as perfectly formed as he'd known they would be after seeing her in the scandalously translucent night shirt she'd worn in Del Rio as casually as if it actually hid her finer assets from view. Now no questions remained. Her nipples were an innocent pink, just as he'd imagined, begging to be teased, ultrasensitive to touch as was every inch of her body.

When he slid out of his clothes and joined her in bed, Bud learned that there are vast differences between fumbling around with a boy who doesn't know what he's doing and making love with a man capable of playing a body like a temperamental string instrument.

She reveled in the feverish heat of his skin, gasping as he pulled at her earlobe with his teeth while she ground her body against his. When his heavy, unwieldy erection slid home between the plump lips of her core, she began to spontaneously shed tears. Partly from the joy of the intimacy they were sharing, finally, and partly from the relief of having him finally be where he belonged. With her. Inside her.

He watched closely, moving slowly with purpose and a concentrated intensity, without questioning her display of emotion.

He knew the wait had been agonizing and antagonizing for both of them. It was also worth it. He'd needed to be sure she knew her mind and was ready for a commitment to a man. She had to be sure he was capable of making a new commitment to life.

He was. They fit together. In every way that counted.

EPILOGUE

Cann took over the business that had originally been his brainchild and was feeling optimistic about ideas for expansion. In March he bought a stone house in Dripping Springs with a big backyard that backed up to a creek and huge mature mesquite trees, the kind that are perfect for climbing.

With the azaleas in full bloom it looked a little like a fairy tale. But it also had a dark side. Cann made sure it had its own state of the art security system that included live feed cameras inside and out. Anytime someone turned the alarm off, any coming or going, he watched the feed on monitors if he was at home, and watched it on his smartphone if he was away. He was also compulsive about making sure Bud's car was in perfect running condition.

Bud didn't mind that his behavior was paranoid sometimes. She understood that we're all just an aggregate result of our experiences.

They got married in their own backyard. The club spared no expense and paid for the entire thing. Bud gave up her job as house mom, but trained her replacement and left the girl wondering if she would ever be able to live up to Bud's standards.

On the last day of May, Bud delivered a little girl, as Cann had predicted. When the new nurse on duty brought the pink bundle of joy into the hospital room, Cann reached out.

"Are you the father?" she asked.

"Yes," he said, as he took Rosebud Dew Johns into the crook of his arm. "This baby is mine."

He and Bud had struggled for months to agree on a name. When she first jokingly suggested Dew as a middle name, in remembrance of the Mountain Dew machine where they met, Cann had laughed. But as time went on, he came to like the idea more and more.

IN SEPTEMBER BUD began matriculating toward a degree from the University of Texas. Cann's business was doing well, but the SSMC still insisted on giving her a scholarship. They claimed that the club did a certain amount of charity every year for tax purposes and that it might as well be her. She was grateful because that meant she could hire someone to stay with Rosie while she was gone to class.

When she thought back over the past eleven months, she was amazed at how much things had changed, in ways she could never have imagined.

Life was strange.

But good.

ALSO BY VICTORIA DANANN

THE KNIGHTS OF BLACK SWAN
Knights of Black Swan 1, My Familiar Stranger
Knights of Black Swan 2, The Witch's Dream
Knights of Black Swan 3, A Summoner's Tale
Knights of Black Swan 4, Moonlight
Knights of Black Swan 5, Gathering Storm
Knights of Black Swan 6, A Tale of Two Kingdoms
Knights of Black Swan 7, Solomon's Sieve
An Order of the Black Swan Novel Prince of Demons
Knights of Black Swan 8, Vampire Hunter
Knights of Black Swan 9, Journey Man

BLACK SWAN, NEXT GENERATION
KBS, Next Generation 1. FALCON: Resistance
KBS, Next Generation 2. JAXON: Repentance
KBS, Next Generation 3. BATISTE: Reliance

THE HYBRIDS
Exiled 1. CARNAL
Exiled 2. CRAVE
Exiled 3. CHARMING

THE WEREWOLVES
New Scotia Pack 1, Shield Wolf: Liulf
New Scotia Pack 2, Wolf Lover: Konochur
New Scotia Pack 3, Fire Wolf: Cinaed

THE WITCHES OF WIMBERLEY
Witches of Wimberley 1; Willem

CONTEMPORARY ROMANCE
Sons of Sanctuary MC, Book 1. Two Princes

Sons of Sanctuary MC, Book 2. The Biker's Brother

Sons of Sanctuary MC, Book 3. Nomad

YOUNG ADULT FANTASY
R. Caine High School, Book 1. The Game Begins: An Introduction

R. Caine High School, Book 2. The Knight

R. Caine High School, Book 3. The High Priestess

Links to all Victoria's books can be found here…
www.VictoriaDanann.com

I sincerely hope you enjoyed reading *NOMAD*.

Reviews are enormously helpful to me. Please take the time to follow a link back to the book you've just read and post your thoughts. A few words are often as powerful as many.

Victoria Danann

NEW YORK TIMES and
USA TODAY BESTSELLING AUTHOR

SUBSCRIBE TO MY PODCAST
Romance Between the Pages

www.romancecast.com

Victoria's Website

victoriadanann.com

Victoria's Facebook Page

facebook.com/victoriadanannbooks

Victoria's Facebook Fan Group

facebook.com/groups/772083312865721

Twitter

twitter.com/vdanann

Pinterest

pinterest.com/vdanann

Printed in Poland
by Amazon Fulfillment
Poland Sp. z o.o., Wrocław